**Here's w'**
**Le,**

# BOOKS BY LESLIE LANGTRY

*Merry Wrath Mysteries:*
Merit Badge Murder
Mint Cookie Murder
Scout Camp Murder
(short story in the Killer Beach Reads collection)
Marshmallow S'More Murder
Movie Night Murder
Mud Run Murder
Fishing Badge Murder
(short story in the Pushing Up Daisies collection)
Motto for Murder
Map Skills Murder
Mean Girl Murder

*Greatest Hits Mysteries:*
'Scuse Me While I Kill This Guy
Guns Will Keep Us Together
Stand By Your Hitman
I Shot You Babe
Paradise By The Rifle Sights
Snuff the Magic Dragon
My Heroes Have Always Been Hitmen
Have Yourself a Deadly Little Christmas (a holiday short story)

*Aloha Lagoon Mysteries:*
Ukulele Murder
Ukulele Deadly

*Other Works:*
Sex, Lies, & Family Vacations

# MAP SKILLS MURDER

a Merry Wrath Mystery

Leslie Langtry

# MAP SKILLS MURDER

# CHAPTER ONE

———

The girl was sound asleep, tucked in her bed, surrounded by stuffed animals. She looked so peaceful. Like an angel. And still, I knew that when she woke up, it would be like poking an outraged wolverine with bedhead.

"*Wake up!*" Five little girls standing around me screamed in unison.

The child leaped out of bed, landing in a defensive stance, a hammer in her right hand. Where had that come from?

"Betty!" Carol Anne, the girl's mother, chastised.

She looked like she thought the girl would hit one of us. I wondered what waking her up for school must be like. Then again, Carol Anne believed she'd been kidnapped by aliens on seven different occasions (aliens who'd taught the woman how to play the bassoon), so who knew what passed for normal in this family?

"What's happening?" Betty shouted as she let the hammer fall to the floor.

"*Kidnap Breakfast!*" the five girls screamed.

"What's a kidnap breakfast?" Betty asked.

We'd only picked up the four Kaitlyns—who'd all spent the night at one house—and Ava, so far. We still had six more stops to make.

The five girls looked at each other curiously.

"I don't know," Ava said. "But it's fun!"

The girls cheered as we collected Betty in her jammies and made our way outside to the van. It was a warm, July night. Actually, it was three o'clock in the morning, and we had more girls to get before dawn.

"Love your pj's," Betty said as she passed me by.

Kelly laughed. Clad in a normal pair of plain blue pajamas, she labored under the impression that my Dora the Explorer jammies were...well, weird.

"I like Dora," I sniffed defensively for the fifth time this evening.

The girls rode with me to Lauren's house, as Kelly followed in her van. When we had all twelve girls, we'd need the other vehicle, since my co-leader didn't like my idea of stacking the girls like bricks in the back.

"Mrs. Wrath?" one of the Kaitlyns asked from the back seat.

No matter how many times I protested, the girls still called me "Mrs." They seemed to think that marriage status wasn't as much a justification for the prefix as just being "older than cancer," as Inez so politely informed me.

"What?" I asked as I maneuvered the car through a dead intersection.

"What are we gonna do when we get to your house?"

"What do you want to do?" I said absently. I wasn't totally sure I knew where Lauren lived. Her family had moved a week before, and I was distracted by the maps app on my cell.

The girls didn't answer because they started bickering about what that answer should be. I wasn't really paying attention, but words like *handcuffs* and *hemlock* floated toward me.

The only house on the block with its porch lights on turned out to be the right place. We unloaded the girls, reminding them to keep quiet. Lauren's mother met us on the front porch and led us inside.

A giant German shepherd approached us, and the girls squealed, gathering around the beast, who immediately dropped to the floor, exposing his belly.

"Girls!" Kelly whispered loudly.

With a collective groan, the kids got up and followed us down the hallway to the little girl's room.

The door opened with a soft creak, and once the first two girls entered, the lights went on and loud death metal music blared from speakers on both sides. I was vaguely aware of something hurtling toward my head, as a tennis ball on a string smacked my forehead.

Lauren sat up, aiming a ping pong ball gun at us. This girl had been prepared. A true Girl Scout. I liked it.

"Lauren!" her mother, Bobbi, cried out. "I told you not to set your traps tonight."

The girl nodded as if it was perfectly normal for a bunch of her friends to appear in her booby-trapped room in the middle of the night.

"Yes you did. But that seemed suspicious. So, I decided *not* to follow that directive."

Kelly narrowed her eyes at me.

I shrugged. "What?"

"This is your doing," she mumbled.

My name is Merry Wrath, and I used to be a spy for the CIA, until the vice president "accidentally" outed me. Since that humiliation, I came back to my hometown of Who's There, Iowa, and started a Girl Scout troop for something to do. After two years with this troop, I was proud of how far these fourth graders had come.

They didn't originally know I'd been a spy, but after some unusual exploits, they'd figured it out. Now these kids embraced everything related to espionage. Despite Kelly's accusation, I was pretty proud of them. Just the week before, Inez and Caterina turned an American Girl doll into a pipe bomb that spewed tiny rubber balls. I'd like to think I had a hand in that—even if I'd tried very hard to convince my co-leader that I hadn't.

"Can we see the snails?" Ava and one of the Kaitlyns asked in unison.

Lauren's house was home to the largest collection of snail paraphernalia in North America, second in the world to a 101-year-old man in Japan. And his collection was different in that all the snails were real, live snails.

"We don't have time for that," Kelly said. "We have to get the Hannahs, Emily, Inez, and Caterina still."

Lauren walked out with us without questioning what was going on—as if she was kidnapped in her pajamas every day.

She and Betty climbed into Kelly's car, and we headed off to pick up the rest of the girls.

"Donuts!" the girls shrieked when we pulled into the parking lot of the local donut shop.

They flooded out of the vans and into the store. As I walked in, several senior citizens, who'd been sitting at the tables inside, looked at each other and without speaking, got up and walked out.

The next few moments were an experiment in madness as each girl called out their favorite donut, simultaneously. Kelly finally calmed them down with the Girl Scout quiet sign—an amazing tactic that worked every time. One by one, each girl announced to the terrified teenager behind the counter, which donuts she liked.

The kid behind the counter, wearing a name tag that read *Reggie*, looked like he'd rather be tied to a tree and swarmed by ravenous squirrels. His Adam's apple bobbed nervously as he tried to fill the order.

I was kind of worried about him, truth be told. The boy was short and so skinny I could practically see through him. Obviously, he didn't eat here. For a moment I wondered why? Was the dough poisoned? Were there rats in the kitchen? My spy-dy senses weren't tingling, so maybe he was just allergic to gluten.

Kelly and I ordered the donuts and paid for them. We collected the boxes from the counter and took everyone back out to the vans and then on to my place.

That was where things got sticky—literally and figuratively. Turned out the girls didn't want to eat the donuts they'd picked, preferring the ones that others had chosen instead. Kelly and I stood back, ready to eat whatever was left. Once the crowd backed off, we found four crullers surrounded by sprinkles and crumbs.

"This is better than what I thought would happen," I said as I devoured my second donut.

Kelly nodded, finishing off her first. "I think it went well."

The whole kidnap breakfast thing was an idea we'd found online. While the troop didn't technically meet over the summer, we tried to come up with something fun to do. One summer it was a trip to Washington, DC. Another year we had a pizza party at the local pool.

And one time we went to a chinchilla farm. Only too late did we discover that the girls had been planning to free the nervous little rodents. Fortunately for us, the animals were so terrified, they huddled together until the farmer scooped them back up.

That was the last time we let Betty and Lauren pick our activity. In fact, that was why Kelly and I decided to come up with something on our own. We were surprised that the parents had no problem waking up and letting us into their homes in the middle of the night.

My cats, Philby (who, through no fault of her own, looked like Hitler) and her kitten Martini (who resembled Elvis), lay in the middle of the sea of girls, who pet them with sticky hands.

I didn't understand why my cats loved these kids so much. Once at a lock-in, they dyed Philby's white fur pink. As if realizing I was thinking about her, Philby shot me a look of contempt before nibbling on a bit of leftover blueberry donut. Narcoleptic Martini fell asleep standing and sort of fell over onto her side.

"Okay, ladies!" Kelly clapped her hands in a two-three-two pattern.

The girls dropped what they were doing and returned the clap. That was a trick Kelly and I also learned online. Between that and the quiet sign, I wondered if we were grooming the troop to be soulless zombies.

But I'd never tell my co-leader that.

"Who wants to play a game?" I shouted.

A cheer erupted that probably woke the rest of the town of Who's There as the girls formed a circle around us. After regaining our hearing, we started the girls on a game of Frog Detective, where one girl was a detective, one was a frog, and the others were all flies. The detective went to another room while the rest decided who's who. When she returned, she stood in the middle of the circle, trying to figure out who the murderous frog was. Meanwhile, the frog was secretly sticking her tongue out at various girls in the circle, "killing" them. They collapsed in death spasms, which with some girls was a bit over the top. The detective had to figure out who the frog was before all the flies were dead.

It was a twisted game. And one of my favorites. If only in the field I could've taken out targets by sticking my tongue out at them. Sigh.

"Come on," Kelly whispered as she dragged me into my kitchen. "We have to get ready for the craft project."

Kelly Albers had been my best friend since elementary school when she helped me take on a bully and discovered that I didn't care that she called me an idiot. When I came back to Who's There to sulk, she was the one with the idea to help the elementary school down the block from my house by forming a Girl Scout troop.

I still haven't figured out if I should be grateful or unforgiving.

Kelly was a nurse at the local hospital, married to Robert, with a baby girl named after me. Her name was Finn. My real name was Fionnaghuala Merrygold Czrygy. When I was outed and my name was all over the news, I took my mother's maiden name and became Merry Wrath—a name that was much easier to say and spell.

I stared down at the glue, glitter, construction paper, and scissors that littered my breakfast bar.

"Are you sure about this?" I asked. "Remember the last time we used glue for something?"

Several months ago, in January, we'd decided to make angel ball ornaments. The idea was to cover a Styrofoam ball in glue and dip it into a bag of white feathers. Somehow the girls got confused or were overly enthusiastic and managed to get the glue all over their arms and hands.

The troop resembled molting chickens. Contrary to popular opinion, some types of glue are not easy to remove. And since I chose a cheap glue that bonds like cement in an ice storm, it was February before the last girl was de-feathered. Kelly blamed me, but the girls loved it. If their parents even noticed, they didn't seem to mind.

"This"—Kelly held up a popular brand—"is the good glue. Now help me set up the table outside."

We dragged two six-foot-long tables and twelve folding chairs out to the backyard. Being that it was July in Iowa, the temperature was in the 80s. I suppose you're wondering how a single woman like me happens to have two folding tables and a dozen chairs?

Because Kelly said I needed them. In hindsight I think it was fair to say I was tricked.

After five minutes we realized that we were outside and the girls were unsupervised inside, and we raced back to the living room.

"Who put lipstick on Philby?" I cried out.

My fat feline führer glared at me with bright red lips, blue eye shadow, giant clip-on earrings, and her hair formed into spikes. Martini was nowhere to be seen. Smart kitty.

"We did makeovers!" Hannah the First said.

"We were just about to do Martini, but we can't find her." The second Hannah pouted.

"Looks like we arrived just in time," Kelly said. "Come on, girls! We're going to make paper-bag masks in the backyard!"

A roar went up, and in seconds the room was empty save for one pissed-off cat. That's when I noticed she was wearing tiny high heels. Where did those come from? Probably one of those American Girl dolls the girls were always talking about.

Why *American* Girl dolls? Were there Paraguayan Girl dolls? Uzbeck Girl dolls? And if there were, it was a devious idea for global domination. Those things were more than $100! I knew this because I'd already bought three for my goddaughter, Kelly's daughter, Finn. Granted, as a toddler, she was a bit young—but I figured I'd stock up ahead of time in case something happened to me. Then she'd remember her godmother fondly as the woman who spoiled her rotten.

I managed to remove the shoes, lipstick, and earrings before Kelly screamed for me from the yard. Philby stormed off, still wearing the eye shadow and spiked hair. I wondered if

Martini would laugh at her mother when she saw her. Oh yes, cats laugh. How do I know? Because mine laugh at me all the time. It's a subtle form of feline human shaming.

Kelly shouted for me to bring paint and markers. I shuddered, but brought my stash. The girls swarmed like flesh-eating beetles.

"How's it going?" I asked my co-leader.

"Okay," Kelly said, but her expression told me she was worried. "It's a good thing we are using safety scissors. Inez started pruning your weeds, and Ava cut the branches off of one of your shrubs."

"They're not weeds…" I grumbled. "I don't have weeds."

"What would you call those?" Kelly pointed at a bed of blooming thistles that stood three feet tall.

Of course, I had weeds. I wasn't much of a landscaper. My fiancé, Rex, who lived across the street, had an immaculate lawn. He enjoyed working outside. I enjoyed watching him. His sweaty biceps and six-pack abs were definitely a bonus.

"That's my Salute to Scotland." I sniffed. Now I could never take those thistles down. It seemed like a bit of a win and a lose.

"And the milkweed?" Kelly pointed at a bunch of plants bearing pods as large as my pets.

"I'm waiting to see if they produce alien copies of me and the cats."

She pointed at the branches of the large tree in the middle of the yard. "And those?"

Twenty-four dead birds hung from the branches from fishing wire. My future sisters-in-law were taxidermists. They presented Rex and me with one stuffed bird for each month we'd known each other. I was just glad they didn't ask me how many months that was. I never was very good at sentimental math.

Philby was pressed up against the kitchen window, paws pasted to the glass. She hated that we didn't bring the birds inside for her to attack.

"Ronni and Randi made them for us. Seemed rude not to hang them up."

Kelly rolled her eyes. "You're so weird."

"What was I supposed to do? They're going to be my family in December."

To be honest, the twins thought they were my family already. Since I'd met them, they...well, Randi (Ronni didn't like me or anyone—I think she was a tad prejudiced against anything living) had presented me with several taxidermied animals, including a giant Maine Coon cat in mid-leap that Philby used as a scratching post. It was a good thing she was declawed.

I'd kept the cat, and a crow named Sigurd doing stand-up comedy, but the rest of them were presently locked up in my guest room. And since it was still riddled with bullet holes from an incident a while back—no one ever went in there.

"What the..." Kelly's exclamation broke into my reverie.

Ava, one of the Hannahs, and Inez were watching Betty dig up my Salute to Scotland.

"Hey!" I shouted as I raced over. "Where'd you get that spade?"

Betty shrugged. "I thought I'd look for buried bodies in your yard."

I narrowed my eyes. "I don't have any bodies buried in my yard." At least, none that I knew of. And I didn't think I had a shovel like that. But then, I was clueless most of the time.

The spade hit something that didn't sound like dirt.

"Whoa! I think I found a casket!" Betty tossed the spade, which narrowly missed me, and got down on her knees.

The other three girls leaned over. I joined them. Betty was brushing dirt off what looked like wood. She'd gotten about two feet down in the dirt. I grabbed the spade and started thrusting it into the dirt to find the edges.

"What are you doing?" Kelly shouted.

"It's a coffin with the remains of an old pioneer pirate who was hung for witchcraft!" Lauren squealed excitedly.

I nodded. "I don't think it's...whatever Lauren just said...but it's something."

Actually, it was a box. About two-foot by one-foot in size. I tugged on it, and it came free, causing me to fall backward with the crate on my chest. Not my most graceful moment. I was surrounded as the other girls joined the circle. Twelve little faces looked down on me, and I wondered for a moment if this wasn't what being the body at a wake was like.

After righting myself, I set the chest down and brushed the rest of the dirt off. It was old. Well, it looked old. I was no historian, but to me the decaying wood and rusted hinges seemed to be at least from the last century.

"It's got a lock on it!" one of the Kaitlyns shouted.

I examined the padlock. The iron was covered in rust, and it looked fairly brittle. I stood up, took aim with the spade I didn't own, and hit it hard. The lock fell apart.

The girls cheered loudly as I opened the box.

"What is it?" Kelly asked.

"Is it a dead dog?"

"Is it a human heart?"

"Is it a human head?"

"Is it a pumpkin carved to look like a wombat?"

The last comment came from Inez, and we looked at her curiously. The girl said nothing more.

"It's way better than that," I said as I pulled the contents up into the air. "It's a treasure map!"

# CHAPTER TWO

———

"It's not a treasure map," Kelly said to the girls.

"Oh yes it is," I said as I gingerly gripped it by the two top corners and carried it over to the tables.

The girls let out an audible gasp as I laid it out. The yellowed page was torn and crumbling, and the writing was a bit blurry. How was it even in this good state after being buried unprotected for so long?

"The Peters Treasure!" Kelly gasped in spite of herself.

Who's There, our town, had been founded by Theobald and his wife, Euphemia. They'd started a lumber mill and bar, and the town sort of grew up around it. And when they died, they left a substantial fortune to their granddaughter Mehitable, which must have been a great disappointment to their grandson Eustace.

Maybe it was her strange name, but Mehitable was considered a bit…off. *She ain't right* was what most local folks wrote in their pioneer diaries (something I'm surprised they even did), about the girl. She never married or had kids. The descendants came from Eustace.

"I always thought it was murder," Kelly mused.

I nodded. "Everyone did."

That was when I noticed a sea of eager faces surrounding us.

"You guys never heard this story?" I asked.

Eleven girls shook their heads. Betty nodded. Of course she knew about it.

"I don't think we should tell the girls," Kelly said.

"It's part of Who's There *history*," I replied. "Those who do not learn from history are doomed to repeat it." I had no idea who said that, but someone important did, and it sounded good.

Kelly rolled her eyes. "I hardly think these girls are going to become axe murderers because they don't know the story."

"*Axe murder?*" the girls cried out collectively.

"Now you did it," I chided my best friend. "You said 'murder' earlier and 'axe murder' now. You really leave me no choice."

The girls were jumping up and down, screaming with joy. I probably should have discouraged it, but I loved this story when I was a kid.

"You guys all know about the Peters, right?"

Twelve hands shot into the air.

"This is about their granddaughter Mehitable. She inherited the family fortune, and her brother, Eustace, did not."

"Well that sucks," Betty interrupted.

I ignored her, because she was right.

"Eustace got married, had kids, and eventually became a very wealthy farmer. Mehitable didn't do any of those things. She got the huge house but never married. For years people saw her on the street, wearing clothes made of meat, or walking a llama. She was kind of like the first Lady Gaga, without the smarts."

"Where'd she get a llama?" Lauren wanted to know.

"That's an excellent question," I said. "And the answer is, I don't know."

"Get to the part about the map," Ava said.

"And the axe murder," Caterina added.

"Okay. Well, Mehitable didn't live too long. She was thirty years old in 1911. And the other residents noticed one day that they hadn't seen her in a while. So a couple of men went to check the house."

I paused for dramatic effect. "They found her in the dining room, with an axe sticking out of her head." I looked at the eager faces around me. "She was dead." Not sure I needed to add that last part.

"*Wow!*" all the girls screamed.

I was starting to wonder if they operated on a hive mind. If that was the case, Betty was definitely the Queen Bee.

"Now you guys may not know it, but there've been a number of axe murders in Iowa. The Villesca House, John Hossack in Indanola. But Mehitable was ours."

Kelly sighed, realizing she was overruled. "Everyone suspected her brother, Eustace, but he had an alibi. He'd been in Texas for a month, buying cattle."

I took over because this was the good part. "The sheriff finally decided that it was a suicide."

The girls looked doubtful. Smart girls.

"I know, right? Anyway, they decided that she'd hit herself in the head with the axe. But before she did, she'd hidden all that money she'd inherited from her grandparents."

"She didn't spend it?" one of the Kaitlyns asked.

Kelly answered. "No. She lived very cheaply. The estimate of how much she had by the time she died was $50,000."

Lauren frowned. "That's not much."

I said, "You might think so, but that much money was the equivalent of one million dollars today."

"They never found the money?" Ava prodded.

"Nope. People thought she hid it in the house, but they looked and never found it there."

Kelly added, "They dug up the yard too, but nothing. And it was weird because she had a will that said she left everything to her llama. And when her llama died, it would all go to Eustace.

"The llama died two weeks later, Kelly continued. The story is that Eustace's family searched the old homestead for years but found nothing. But since he was already wealthy in his own right, he gave up, and that was the end of that."

My eyes turned back to the map. "Some folks thought she buried the money. But after a while, people moved on."

Ava rubbed her chin. "Would paper money from the olden days be worth the same money today?"

"That's a good question. But the gossip was, because she never used the bank in town, that it was gold bullion and she'd buried it herself."

I'd always loved this story as a kid. Kelly and I had ridden our bikes around town, hoping to find a gold bar sticking out of the ground.

We never did.

"We should find the treasure." Betty smacked her fist.

"I think we should solve her murder," Lauren suggested.

The girls divided up, taking sides, and while they debated, Kelly and I took another look at the map.

"MP." I pointed to the initials in the lower right-hand corner. "It has to be her."

"The town plat here looks like it did one hundred years ago." Kelly squinted. "But if it's a map, where's the big *X*?"

She had a point. A line wove through the town, winding around houses and crossing back over itself multiple times. And then it faded to nothing. I held it up to the sun, but couldn't see it. I turned it over. On the back was a hand-drawn picture of a llama. Yup. Definitely hers.

"Mehitable's Map." Kelly shook her head. "People have been looking for that thing for one hundred years. And it was in your backyard all this time. The question is, why is it in your yard?"

I shook my head. "No clue." To be honest, I was a little freaked out by that.

Kelly asked, "Do you think the treasure is here too?"

I shook my head. "There'd be no need for a map if the treasure was right here." I thought about this for a second. "There's one place we should check first."

Kelly's eyes grew wide. "You're really going to look for the treasure?"

"Of course. Why? Did you think I was kidding?"

She looked at me for a long while and then sighed. "I guess not. So what's the one place we should check first?"

"Her house. And I just so happen to know the owners."

# CHAPTER THREE

———

The kidnap breakfast had been a success. After the girls and Kelly had gone, my cell went off. I couldn't help but smile.

"Randi! I was just thinking of you!" I went to pick up a paper bag, and it was surprisingly heavy. Philby was inside, giving me the stink eye, as if to say *How dare you! You can't see me!*

"Really? Well, I was just calling because I have an idea for your wedding! Can you come over in the morning?"

"Absolutely." I hung up.

For the past month, since I'd met her for the first time, Randi had made suggestions for the wedding décor on a regular basis. A replica wedding diorama made of dead kittens…two mice dressed as the bride and groom for the top of the cake…a photo of me, in my dress, surrounded by happy woodland creatures playing instruments…and dead fish in the punch bowls.

These ideas terrified me, mostly because I wondered how she was going to get thirty dead kittens for the diorama, and I was pretty sure dead fish in the punch wasn't exactly a hygienically sound idea.

Randi had assured me that the kittens died from natural causes, which made me wonder exactly what they had in their basement. I imagined a large chest cooler filled with animals in baggies. How did you get thirty kittens who died of natural causes, anyway?

The hardest part was finding a way to turn her down without upsetting her. By some small miracle, I'd managed so far. But sooner or later I knew I'd have to give in.

The next morning Rex dropped by, surprising me with one dozen donuts and an intimate smile that always made me a little weak in the knees. Some people think that the way to a woman's heart is with diamonds or flowers. With me, it's any cake-like substance. It's possible I might have a problem.

"By the way," I said through a mouthful of donuts. "Your sisters have another idea for the wedding. I'm heading over there next. Any special requests? Maybe an elephant as the best man or a ring-tailed lemur as the ring bearer?"

Rex shook his head as he pulled me against him. "How about nothing dead at our wedding?"

"I'm working on it." I really was. But the twins never seemed to hear those words when I said them.

"Good luck!" He kissed me in a way that suggested there was more to come later.

With a naughty little wink, he walked out the door.

Randi and Ronni Ferguson operated their business out of the old Peters House on Main Street. The first house built in town, it was a lovely Victorian with lots of bric-a-brac and gingerbread. Sadly, that did not mean the house was edible. And yes, I asked.

Since they'd moved in, the women had fixed up the house, painting it in bright colors with special attention to detail. The exterior of the old house had been fully restored to its original nineteenth-century glory. Inside was another matter.

As I entered, the doorbell rang out with the sound of dogs barking. It was a nice replacement for the original, which had sounded like a gunshot and had always sent me into a nosedive.

"Merry?" Randi shouted from the back. "I'll be out in a minute!"

The inside of the house looked like an after-hours party in the magic forest of a deranged wizard. Animals of every make and model were either posed in mid-pounce or turned into something resembling people doing peopley stuff.

On my right, two warthogs in overalls were entrenched in a fierce game of checkers. In front of me, two mountain lions played Twister while wearing bunny suits. On my left was a dozen squirrels fleeing a Godzilla-like Great Dane on a rampage through the countryside.

The most amazing thing about this place was that this stuff *sold*. Every time I was in here, they had all new dioramas. Randi said that they did a lot of online business and that the basement was full of work waiting to be displayed. Ronni threatened me with a deceased flamingo when I asked if I could go down there. It was never a good idea to upset a crazy woman armed with waterfowl.

How was it possible that Rex turned out so normal, considering that his sisters were so…um…eccentric? Could it be that their estrangement had something to do with it? Should I thank the twins for that?

A noise on my left made me turn with a smile, only to find a scowling Ronni, her arms crossed over her chest, clearly planning my demise. I wondered how she'd stuff me. My demented brain came up with all sorts of unseemly ideas.

"Oh, hi, Ronni," I said with as much enthusiasm as I could muster.

"Stop distracting Randi with all your stupid wedding requests!" she growled. "We've got seven badgers in the back for a special order with the University of Wisconsin, and we're not done with it."

Correcting her and insisting that these wedding *things* were all Randi's ideas would do no good, because I'd told her many times over. For some reason, Ronni wanted me to be the bad guy.

"Okay" was all I said. It was all I ever said because it always seemed to appease her and make her leave the room.

"Merry! My favorite sister-in-law to be!" Randi joined me, holding something covered in a cloth.

I hugged her because she liked it when I did that. As an only child, I figured this kind of thing was required. For years the twins and their baby brother, Rexley, had been estranged due to some unfortunate incident with a dead armadillo. I wasn't sure exactly what happened, because none of them would explain any further. Apparently, when angry, Ronni's modus operandi was the liberal application of deceased critters.

A few months back I'd reunited the brother and his sisters. I was kind of proud of that. Rex had never really thanked me for it, but I knew deep down he was kind of, sort of happy.

"Now Merry…" Randi's face was flushed with excitement.

Here we go…

"Keep an open mind, but I have a great idea!"

She always called terrible ideas great ones. Maybe she had some sort of weird dyslexia. I was waiting for the day when she told me she'd had a terrible idea—even if I wasn't sure I wanted to know what that idea would be.

"You need a garter to toss, so I came up with this." She whipped the cloth off the thing in her hand.

I gasped, which she took to mean that I loved it.

"Praying mantids? For my garter?"

Four very large, very dead praying mantids were attached foot to—um—forearm, to form a ring that would apparently go around my thigh. Each one wore a tiny wedding veil, and as a testament to her talent, they all seemed to be smiling.

"Do you," I said slowly, "think this might give off the wrong message? I mean, don't mantids bite their husbands' heads off after sex? It would be a short wedding night."

The short, plump brunette's face fell, and she stared at the creatures. "I hadn't thought of that."

Most people would have tried to cheer the woman up, but I'd had lots of practice. I waited until she burst into a huge smile seconds later.

"That's okay, because I have a really great idea I've been holding back!"

She always said that. Randi was very creative with an endless well of ideas for putting dead animals into weird situations. She handed me the mantids chain.

"Take it anyway," she said. "You can wear it on your head for the rehearsal dinner!" Randi clapped her hands in glee.

I turned the ring of bugs around in my hands. "Isn't it a bit fragile?"

My future sister shook her head. "I reinforced them with wire and a lot of superglue. I'd better get back to work. I should have the perfect thing in a day or two!"

Ronni appeared, looking more furious than usual. Which was saying a lot.

"What is it?" Randi's voice softened at the sight of her sister.

"Mail!" her twin shrieked.

I'd never heard anyone scream the word *mail* with the hostility you'd usually reserve for a Chechen terrorist, or that bag boy at the store who dumps a watermelon on top of your bananas (I really hate that guy).

"Excuse me, Merry. We have a small issue to deal with. Come back soon!"

Randi ran off into the back, and I nosed around the house. This had been the home of Mad Mehitable (or Mad Mimi, as she was known). History said the house had been virtually taken apart by her brother, Eustace, when she died. If that was true, there'd be no point in searching here.

Still, it was always smart to start from the beginning. The dozens of glass-eyed animals blocked me from most of the walls, but what I could get to seemed legit. The drywall was old. Maybe the twins had noticed something. If they had, would they tell Rex, or keep it to themselves?

And while I wouldn't put that past Ronni, I was sure Randi would've said something had she found a million dollars in gold bullion. What would they have spent it on? I wondered. Several horrifying ideas popped into my head, and I decided not to pursue that avenue of thinking.

Hopefully, the sisters wouldn't realize I was still here. I moved very carefully through the parlor and out into the hallway. The creaking floorboards reminded me that the twins hadn't done anything to the interior. The ceilings had water stains on them.

I thought of the map and wondered if that flimsy piece of paper was all a ruse to hide the fact that the money was inside the house? People said Eustace looked for it and went away empty-handed. I'd think he would've been very motivated to find his grandparents' money.

Maybe I wasn't looking at the puzzle clearly. Maybe I should start with why the Peters had cut their grandson out of the will.

I opened the door, realizing too late that the alarm would go off. I hightailed it to my car and was out of there before Ronni found out I'd lingered.

The Who's There Historical Society was just a few blocks down the street, in a little log cabin they claimed was the first building Theobald Peters had built when he'd founded the town. It was a possibility that this was true, but most people thought he'd lived in the lumber mill, because *that* was the first thing he'd built.

I opened the rough-hewn door and went inside. The cabin had only one room, but every single surface was covered with books, papers, and old photos. Filing cabinets stood against a wall and in the center of the room, and an elderly lady in a flower print blouse and cardigan was sitting at a table, studying a piece of paper. She didn't seem to notice me.

"Hello," I said quietly.

The woman jumped, her hand fluttering to her heart. "Oh! You startled me!"

She took a few deep breaths, regained her composure, and smiled. "I'm Edna Lou Murphy. I'm the president of the Who's There Historical Society. Are you in the wrong place?"

I was about to say it would be unlikely for anyone to walk into a log cabin with a huge sign that said *Historical Society*, if I'd been looking for something else. But she seemed nice, so I didn't.

Edna Lou stood about five foot five and was thin. White hair was piled in a bun on top of her head, and she wore a skirt with nylons and sensible shoes. Her shoulders were a little stooped, but her smile was warm and welcoming. I liked her immediately.

"Merry Wrath," I said. "I grew up here."

Uh-oh. I shouldn't have said that. I was still a little incognito, although the word was probably getting around about who I really was. After two years of living here, the police and my Girl Scouts were figuring it out. I probably should've retired somewhere else, like What Cheer, Iowa.

Edna squinted at me. "Are you related to Adelaide Wrath?"

I nodded. "She was my grandmother."

Wrath was my mother's maiden name. Her mother, Adelaide, had had a farm outside of town. She'd been an amazing woman who wasn't afraid of anything and had kept a loaded shotgun behind the kitchen door "just in case." I'd once asked her what she meant by that, but she didn't answer. She never drank or swore and made the best apple pie this side of the Mississippi.

As fierce as she was, it was no surprise when she died in her late nineties while chopping down a tree. Apparently, the kitten had gotten stuck up in the branches, and she couldn't be bothered to get the ladder. Her dying words to my mother when asked why she didn't use a ladder were, "Are you crazy? Those things are dangerous!"

"You must be Judith's daughter?" Edna frowned.

She was right. My mother was an only child. So was I. And I hated it.

"You're Finn Czrygy! The spy!" She clapped her hands together with glee.

I guess I should've known I wouldn't be able to put one over on a historical researcher.

I winced. "That's right. But most people here think I'm Merry Wrath, and I'd kind of like to keep it that way."

"Of course. I won't tell a soul." She gave me a jolly wink.

Edna pushed a plate of cookies toward me, and I took one, because duh! Cookies!

"Why are you here, Merry?"

"My Girl Scout Troop is working on a project where they need to know the town's history," I lied.

"That's wonderful!" Edna squeaked. "So few young people are interested in local history anymore."

I nodded. "I've always found the town lore fascinating. Are all the Peters gone now?"

Edna shook her head. "All gone. Poor souls. Each one died young." She looked at a photo on the wall of a glowering man with enormous bushy eyebrows who seemed to stare directly at me. "Peter Peters died in the '60s."

"What happened to him?" I was trying not to make eye contact with the photo or ask why he had such a repetitive name.

"He drowned while swimming in Lake Okoboji."

"That's too bad…"

She shook her head. "He didn't know how to swim. Stubborn man. Refused help even after he went under. Twice."

"Really?" I hadn't heard about that.

"Oh, yes, dear. I was there. Saw the whole thing. You couldn't tell a Peters what to do."

For just a moment I thought about pressing her for the whole story, but decided I really didn't want to hear it.

"Who's There has such an interesting story, with pioneers, a mysterious murder, and a hidden treasure." I tried to sound nonchalant. "The girls have been eating it up. I just wish I knew more to tell them."

Edna Lou pulled out a chair for me. As I sat, she pulled a file from one of the cabinets and sat across from me.

"Mehitable Peters." She handed me a photo, and it took all my self-control not to jump.

The woman in the photo looked a lot like me—if I were crazy with long, wild hair and no eyelids. She must have been in her thirties, dressed in a clown costume, and barefoot. And the picture looked like it had been taken in a studio, due to the painted background. Mehitable's eyes were wide as she stared at the camera. Her mouth was in a tight line. Long, dark hair looked like it hadn't been combed in a month. It was thick and stuck out from her head as if she'd just been electrocuted.

If Edna noticed a similarity, she didn't say it. "She was twenty-eight when this was taken. It was her llama's birthday, so she decided to commemorate the moment with a photograph. This is one of only a few pictures we have of her."

"It was her llama's birthday, and she had her picture taken?" How did she know the birth date of her llama?

The woman nodded and pulled out another photo. "This is her brother, Eustace, around the same time."

This picture looked normal. A handsome man in his thirties, with his wife and children. They were dressed to the nines in the same studio with the same backdrop. He didn't look anything like his sister, but maybe that was because he was cleaned up and she was, well…not. Eustace looked relaxed in his suit and wore a glorious mustache.

"What can you tell me about Mehitable?"

Edna looked thoughtful for a moment, as if trying to access something in a filing cabinet in her brain.

"Mehitable's family called her Mimi. We have her diary. She was a normal little girl who wrote a lot about her life. It wasn't until she turned twenty-six that she lost her senses."

"Have you read her diary?"

Edna walked back to the cabinet and returned with an old, leather-bound book. I flipped loosely through it. From this brief browsing, it seemed that the first couple of hundred pages featured her life from age seven to twenty-six. There were mentions of dolls, her father at the family lumber mill or tavern, her mother's lard sandwiches…normal stuff for that era, I guessed.

I flipped to the last page with writing. It was on her twenty-sixth birthday. Only one word was on the page.

*Wubble.*

"You should publish this." I handed it back.

Edna nodded. "I'd love to. Maybe someday."

I was pretty sure she shouldn't wait. Edna Lou Murphy didn't look like she had a lot of somedays left.

"It looks like she snapped on her birthday," I said. "The page before talks about making butter."

"Yes. That's what all of us think too."

I looked around the room, wondering if at any second I was going to have old people jumping out at me. "All of you?"

"The historical society. Well, me and my cousin Ike. The others have died off over the years. I'm the only one keeping it going. I keep saying 'all of us' out of habit."

I made a mental note to give a large donation to the society. "You said her grandparents—what about her parents?"

Edna looked to her right, and then to her left, before leaning in. "It was just her mother. No one ever knew who the father was." She looked over her glasses at me. "Winifred died when Mimi was only two." She leaned closer and whispered, "Consumption."

I nodded as if I knew what the hell that meant. "So, Mimi and Eustace's grandparents raised them?"

"Oh yes. And when they died, they left everything to Mimi."

I had to ask, "How did Theobald and Euphemia Peters die?"

"It was an accident. They were driving in their carriage, and something spooked the horse. He reared up, and Euphemia was thrown. Her neck was broken. As Theobald struggled to control the horse, he fell out of the carriage. He died two days later."

The questions kept bubbling up on my lips, and I realized I really was fascinated. "Why did they give all of their money to Mimi?"

Edna searched through the file and brought out a piece of paper in a plastic sleeve. It was the last will and testament of Theobald and Euphemia Peters and looked as though it would disintegrate if anyone so much as looked at it. There were only a few sentences, including one that left everything to their granddaughter. Their grandson wasn't even mentioned.

"Something must've happened," I mumbled.

"Oh yes," Edna agreed. "There have been many theories over the years. The town was pretty divided over it. Half of the town believed it was a forgery, while the other half figured that because Eustace was doing well and Mimi was getting a little soft in the head, they left the money for her care."

"How did Eustace feel about that?"

She shrugged. "Everything I've seen on the subject implies that he took it well. People were impressed with how he handled it."

And now, literally, the million-dollar question, "How did Mimi spend her inheritance?"

Edna thought for a moment. "I've found old receipts that indicate she had standing orders for groceries and other sundries. They were delivered to her until she died. Besides the llama, every other expenditure seemed okay."

The girls would never forgive me if I didn't ask about the llama. "Where did she get the llama?"

"Her grandparents visited Peru. No one really knows why. But they brought her a llama. His name was Tinkles."

"And the fabled treasure?" I ventured.

Edna laughed. "That has been a legend since the day Mimi died. She didn't leave a will. Oh, there were rumors that she left it all to Tinkles, but I haven't seen any proof of that. What was left in her accounts took care of her bills around town with the grocer, at the feed store, and the like. Eustace bought the house at auction and spent years looking through it. He never found the money."

How could she have hidden it? And where? "It was a considerable fortune, like a million dollars, right?"

"Yes. She had it all in gold bullion. Not an easy thing to hide. But no one ever found it. As disturbed as she was, it's possible she gave it away or lost it."

I thought about this. Edna tidied up the files but left the diary and two photos behind.

"Could I make copies of the pictures?" I asked.

The woman took them over to a printer and returned with two copies. That was nice of her.

"How does the Historical Society support its studies?"

"We have a very small grant from the city. Mayor Scott has been generous enough to keep it going," Edna said. "I'm a volunteer and the only staff. Money is running a little short. I'm thinking of writing a few proposals to foundations in the area."

The expression on her face told me she didn't have a lot of confidence in that idea.

I pulled out my checkbook and wrote a check for one thousand dollars and handed it to her. Rex would probably frown on this. I was a bit of an impulse spender. But I'd gotten a huge settlement from the CIA when they kicked me out for the outing that wasn't my fault. Besides, Edna Lou needed it more than I did. And it made me feel good to help out.

"A small donation," I said. "I might have a connection or two for state funding." I was thinking of my father, Senator Michael Czrygy. While he was in the US Senate now, he still had a lot of influence in the state house.

Edna's jaw dropped. "Not only are you the only person who's visited this place in years, you're the only donor!"

"That's going to change. I'm going to mobilize my Girl Scout troop to help out. You come up with a list of things you need, and we will make it happen."

Where did this charitable Merry Wrath come from? I liked her!

Tears formed in Edna's eyes, and she threw her frail arms around my midsection. She was so frail it felt like a light breeze. I gave her my phone number and insisted she call me.

"Someday…" She wiped her tears on a tissue she'd pulled from her sleeve. "I'm going to get the Peters House and turn it into a museum!"

"What?" I asked. The house Randi and Ronni lived and worked in?

Edna nodded. "Oh yes! It's always been my dream to do that. We can't let Villisca get all the glory!"

All the glory? Villisca was a small town about an hour and a half away. In 1912 an entire family and two guests were murdered in their sleep. No one was ever apprehended, and it remained a mystery to the present day. The house is now a museum. And apparently, Edna thought they unfairly reaped some benefit from what had happened there. I wondered if Edna was related to Betty?

"Our axe murder is just as important as theirs! Sure, it was only one person, but that's just as sad! They turned the Lizzie Borden house into a bed-and-breakfast, you know. A bed-and-breakfast! The Peters Home would be perfect for that!"

"Um"—my tongue twisted as I tried to find the words— "isn't there a business there now?"

But Edna Lou wasn't listening. "We even have the axe that killed her! Can't you imagine it over the mantel in the parlor?" Her eyes brimmed with joy.

"Yeah, well…"

"And those outsiders swooped in and took the house before I could come up with the down payment." She dabbed her eyes again. "But this"—she waved my check at me—"this will help because I've got a lawyer working on it."

Time to go… "Well, thank you. I'll get the girls to come with me next time."

As I walked out the door, Edna shouted, "Wait!"

She handed me Mehitable's diary. "Just be very careful with it," Edna said. "I think you'll find it interesting."

Tucking the journal into my purse, I thanked her and left the little cabin.

On the way to my car, I wondered, did I just finance a plan to evict my future sisters-in-law? Maybe I'd keep that to myself…

# CHAPTER FOUR

——————

"What are you reading?" Rex joined me in the backyard and pulled up a lawn chair.

"The diary of a madwoman," I mumbled.

Rex handed me a glass of wine and set the bottle down on a little table between us. He was truly the perfect man—always anticipating my needs before I knew what I needed. And right now, I needed a glass of wine.

"I think I've heard of that," Rex said after a hello kiss that made my knees go all rubbery. My fiancé was a terrific kisser. His lips spoke volumes, and had I not been currently enthralled with a crazy woman, I might have dragged him inside for a little make-out session.

I shook my head. "That's not the title. It's actually Mehitable Peters' diary."

Rex was a transplant to Who's There, so he was not a Whorish. You read that right. Natives call themselves Whorish—pronounced *hooreesh*—an unfortunate mixing of *Who's* and *Irish* (for the majority of settlers who moved here mid-eighteenth century). Whoever came up with that didn't really think it through, and we always regret it at the infamous high school football game against our rivals from Bladdersly (their only opportunity to make fun of someone else's name because they are the *Raging Bladders*).

So I filled him in on this little bit of our history. My fiancé let me tell the whole thing and didn't even interrupt. Not even once. He even refilled my glass—which was a bonus for me.

"Wubble?" he asked when I was done.

"Yup. I think she was murdered. Edna Lou Murphy at the Historical Society said it was classified as an accident, but I've role-played it a little, and it just doesn't seem to work." I nodded behind me.

Over in the corner of the patio, Philby lay on her side, a fake axe-through-the-head headband on. She'd refused to let me take it off. She lay there like a proper victim. Good kitty.

The corners of Rex's lips twitched. "So, Philby was Mimi?"

"She played her role very well." At the sound of my voice, Martini trotted out from behind a planter, dressed as a llama.

"I just don't see," I continued, "how it's possible to fall on an axe with your head."

"But you don't know that's what really happened." Rex scooped up the kitten and removed the llama suit. Martini passed out in the middle of the process, so he held her on his lap.

I shrugged. "All the historical society has is her diary, the will, and these photos." I handed him the pictures that Edna Lou had copied for me.

Rex's eyes grew wide when he saw Mehitable. He looked from me to her and back to me.

"She looks like you. If you were insane, that is."

"I think so too. Are you into that? Because I have a clown suit somewhere…"

Rex laughed. "Not really. And the costume is a definite turnoff."

Well, now I knew what I wasn't going as for Halloween.

He flipped through the diary and read a passage here and there as he skimmed. "She died in the old Peters House? Where my sisters now live?"

I decided not to tell him of Edna's plan to turn the taxidermy shop into an axe murder B&B. "That's right."

We sat for a few moments, him thinking, me drinking. Martini woke up and spotted a butterfly. She raced around the yard, chasing it, fell asleep in mid-jump, and dropped to the grass like a sack of cat litter.

"Do you think I should take her to the vet?" I asked Rex.

He looked at the kitten, whose legs were twitching.

"Maybe you should call Dr. Alvarez. But later. I have an idea."

I liked his ideas. They usually started with pizza and ended with a make-out session.

"The Who's There Police Department has only been in existence since the 1920s. But the county sheriff's department has been around much longer. I could see if they have the files on her death, or murder. I'm sure they wouldn't mind us looking at them."

I sat straight up. "Us? You mean you and me?"

Rex nodded. "For once, I'll work on this with you. It might be fun to try to solve a cold case."

I jumped from my chair and climbed into his lap, kissing him furiously.

He pulled back for a breath of air. "So it's a yes?"

I nodded. "When can we go see the sheriff?"

\* \* \*

Sheriff Ed Carnack met us the next day. Rex called in to the police station and told them he was taking a vacation day, which was fine because he was between cases at the moment, and aside from a shoplifting at the gas station and the breakup of a teenage kegger party, nothing much was going on.

"That's a famous case. I always wondered if it really was an accident." The sheriff was a big man with an easy smile. I'd had to work with him (sort of) on a case the past spring.

Who's There was the county seat, and so the sheriff's department was located in town.

"We have files that go back to the late 1800s. It might take a day to find them, but why not?"

He promised to call us the minute he knew anything. That was when I thought about the library.

"They would have old newspaper records, right?"

Rex frowned. "They should. If the town newspaper doesn't go back that far, I'll bet the *Des Moines Register* does."

\* \* \*

Microfiche. Why did it have to be *microfiche*? I hate microfiche. I thought these thoughts as a blonde, buxom librarian named Genevieve (at least, that was the name on her tag) set us up in the back of the library with a box of the little films.

I never understood the allure of microfiche. I never was able to scan them quickly on those machines. In the movies and on TV, they race through them, the screen a blur, until the hero stops at just the right spot. I never knew a spy who could do that, and I knew some pretty talented secret agents.

Microfilm was the spy trick du jour during the Cold War. We had to train in its use at the Farm, and I hated it. These days we can take pictures with our phones and text them to the powers that be way faster than developing film and hiding it in a hollowed-out shoe heel.

Rex loaded the machine and started scrolling at the date of Mehitable's death. He was right. The local paper didn't even exist back then. The paper in the big city of Des Moines, thirty miles away, covered rural news.

"Here it is." Rex stopped on a page. "The date is two days after the murder. But I suspect that's because it took a while to report these things."

Mehitable, or Mimi Peters, filled the screen. This photo was different from the one I had. It must've been taken in her early twenties. She looked serene in a white lace blouse, with her hair pinned up in the style of that time.

And she looked a lot like me.

"Are you sure you aren't related?" Rex asked. "You could be twins."

"Grandma Wrath never mentioned it. And I didn't know Dad's parents. He never was one for genealogy. I'm sure Mom or Dad would've known if we were Peters descendants."

"Must be a fluke." Rex squinted at the screen as he brought up the news story.

*PETERSTOWN HEIRESS DIES IN FREAK ACCIDENT*

*July 1, 1911, Peterstown, IA. Mehitable Peters, or Mimi, as she was known, was found on June 29th, dead in her home. The inquest determined that the heiress to the Peters fortune had slipped and fallen on an axe in her dining room. Cause of death—blunt force trauma to the head. Neighbors seemed relieved and sad at the woman's passing.*

I leaned over Rex's shoulder, "That's it? That's all they have?"

"That's some shoddy police work," my fiancé said. "I guess it's possible to trip and land on an axe, but why would anyone have an axe in their dining room?"

I shrugged. "She was considered very eccentric. Don't you think it's sad, and odd that the neighbors were relieved?"

"The mentally ill, back in those days, if they had money, were allowed to live in their own homes. Who knows what she got up to? Maybe her llama had terrorized the neighborhood?"

"If she was so famous, why didn't they write more in the paper?" It seemed sad that this woman's whole life was summed up in one bizarre accident. Or murder.

Rex scanned the rest of the front page. "There was a lot of news that day. Look here—a horse-theft ring was captured, a group of vigilantes kidnapped a suspected murderer and strung him up outside the courthouse, and some cow gave birth to two two-headed calves. They wouldn't have had much room to write about an accident."

"Vigilantes?" My right brow went up.

Rex nodded. "Oh sure. It was still kind of the Wild West out here. And even though there were lawmen, it wasn't uncommon for a mob to take the law into their own hands before a jury ever saw the case."

My mouth dropped open. "You're joking."

He shook his head. "Nope. And when it came time to find the vigilantes, people went face blind. They wouldn't turn their neighbors in. In fact, they often thanked them for their service to the community."

"Huh," I mumbled. "I never thought of Iowa as the Wild West before."

"Look." Rex pointed at the screen.

A week later there was a story about Eustace Peters moving into his sister's house. He stood beside the building, looking stern.

"The house looks the same," I mused.

Rex nodded. "My sisters renovated the outside for authenticity."

"So what do you think, Detective? Accident or murder?"

Rex leaned back in his chair and stared into space. "I'm going to go with murder. And I'm going to guess that the marshal called it an accident just to avoid dealing with an investigation."

Edna Lou would like that. She hoped it was a murder so the Historical Society could make something big out of it. I understood that. Besides the world's second-largest snail collection, there wasn't much else of interest in this town.

We spent the afternoon going through the rest of the microfiche files but found nothing more. By the time we got back to my house, I was starving.

Rex ran over and grabbed a couple of steaks from his fridge, and I opened a bottle of wine. As the meat sizzled on the grill, I remembered the map.

We laid it out on the table.

"Do you really think there's a treasure?" Rex asked.

"I don't know. I don't even know how it got into this yard."

"Show me where you found it."

We studied the hole but found nothing unusual. I still had the decaying wooden box, but that led nowhere. As Rex turned the steaks, I ran my hands over it. There weren't any identifying features. Nothing that said this box belonged to anyone in particular.

"We should ask Edna Lou about the history of this neighborhood," Rex offered. "That should tell us something."

"That's an excellent idea." I turned the map over and showed him the drawing of the llama. It was a decent job. Mad Mimi had some talent.

"I've never seen a map without a treasure before. And the last word in her diary before she went mad, that is, was *wubble*. What do you think it means?" I asked.

Rex stared at them for a while before getting the steaks off the grill. As we ate, I couldn't help wonder what had really happened, all those years ago, that made Mehitable crazy. Granted, there was a lot of lead poisoning, medicines were a dicey prospect at best, and sometimes people just lost their minds. But still, what changed in one day when she was twenty-six Why did she write about dull household chores one day and *Wubble* the next?

Grabbing my cell, I looked up the meaning of the word *Wubble*. There was only one definition. The *Urban Dictionary* said: *To insert a tentacled appendage into the ocular oriface of a victim, impregnating their skull with squid eggs.*

I shared this information with Rex. He choked on his steak. After a hard pat on the back, he was better.

"What did you say?" He coughed and downed a glass of water.

"It's just like it says," I repeated. "An octopus or squid sticks a tentacle into something's eye socket, knocking up its skull."

My fiancé stared at me.

"Saying it out loud doesn't make it sound any better, I guess." I toyed with the idea that maybe Randi and Ronni would know what this means. But decided not to mention it to Rex.

"And they didn't have the *Urban Dictionary* back then," I said. "It most likely meant nothing…a nonsense word."

"Not necessarily," Rex countered. "It could be code. Or a nickname. It could mean something we haven't thought of."

That was the detective talking.

"What do we do now?" I said after polishing off my steak. "We've hit the sheriff for records and the library and the newspaper."

Rex shrugged. "She died more than 100 years ago, so there probably aren't any witnesses or suspects living."

I picked up the diary. "We have this. I'll keep reading and see if there is anything."

We finished our dinner in silence. Not an uncomfortable or awkward silence, but the kind of silence brought about by too much thinking. Even though we hadn't found anything conclusive, we'd made a pretty serious start. And that was something.

"You know what?" Rex pulled me against him as we cleared the table. "I like investigating with you."

"Of course you do. I'm amazing." I pushed him back playfully.

"Not so fast." Rex pulled me back into his arms and held me tight. "I don't know if it's the squid tentacles, but this case has given me all sorts of ideas."

His lips pressed against mine. This was an unexpected perk of investigating together. The dishes never did get done as we explored a new avenue of *investigation* on the couch.

After a while, I kissed him good night, and sadly, he headed home. I ignored the dishes again and brought the diary to bed with me. Maybe somewhere between butter churning and llama husbandry, I'd find something that provided a clue, other than skull-impregnating squid tentacles.

# CHAPTER FIVE

———

I'd like to say that Mehitable's diary was riveting reading that kept me up all night. I'd like to say that—but it wouldn't be true. The woman's life, or at least her record of it, was boringly mundane, peppered with a few things here or there that made me wonder if her madness hadn't started a little earlier.

She wrote at length about each and every household chore, from hand washing the family's laundry, to hanging it on the line, to feeding the chickens, to sewing. And the strange thing was, they were wealthy enough to have at least two maids.

Perhaps Mimi found comfort in the little things. Maybe doing all this stuff when she didn't need to was what drove her mad. All I know was, it made me fall asleep.

The alarm on my cell woke me up at noon. A couple of weeks ago, I'd had mind-crushing insomnia. Now I slept for hours. Originally, planning the wedding had made me a nervous wreck. But now that almost everything was organized, I felt comfortable enough to sleep.

Philby looked up, still wearing the hatchet-through-the-head gag. Fat and sassy, with her uncomfortable resemblance to Hitler, this cat made my life interesting. And that was saying something.

I found Martini in the hallway, on her back, legs splayed and fast asleep. Maybe I should get her into the vet. But then, I'd read somewhere that cats spend 80 percent of their day sleeping, so perhaps I should leave it alone.

After a quick shower and a couple of Pop-Tarts, I decided to head back to the historical society's cabin for another chat with Edna Lou. I wasn't finished with the diary yet, but maybe my visit had jogged her memory and she'd have some more insights for me.

It was a beautiful day, unseasonably cool for July. Usually we were sizzling at this point, but not today. I wasn't complaining. At the park, I got out of the car and headed for the little log cabin.

When I was a kid, the log cabin had been closed. It was such a fixture in the city park, I barely noticed it. Had the historical society been using it back then? That was a possibility. I probably should've shown an interest before now, but it was more likely I was too busy spinning on the merry-go-round until I threw up.

Looking toward that bit of equipment, I saw that a familiar patch of ground near it was devoid of grass. I must not have been the only one.

Edna Lou knew my grandmother and mother. How did I not know her? Murphy…it was a popular name in town. We'd had a lot of Irish settlers back in the nineteenth century. I knew of at least three Murphy families. She and her cousin must belong to at least one of them.

I tested the doorknob, wondering if it was open, and it gave way. I stepped inside and was immediately assailed with the smell of copper. I knew that smell. That was a bad smell.

The lights were off, so I switched them on. I wished I hadn't.

A pair of legs stuck out from under the table, and there were bloodstains on the far wall. I suppressed a shudder. I'd seen a number of bodies over the years, but what if this was Edna? I liked Edna.

"Edna Lou? Are you okay?" I asked. Because of what I'd found, why did I think this person would answer?

Taking my cell out of my pocket, I dialed 9-1-1 and told the dispatcher what was going on. Then I walked around the table.

A very old man lay there, unmoving. An axe lay on the floor next to him. Just to make sure he wasn't still alive, I reached down and checked his pulse. Nope. This guy was gone. Murdered. And I was the one who found the body. Some things never changed.

The door opened, and I saw Edna Lou's silhouette in the doorway. I lunged for her, dragging the woman outside, and closing the door behind us.

"What is going on?" the woman asked. "Where's Ike?"

"Ike?" I asked in a poor attempt to stall. The sirens were already closing in.

"My cousin." Edna's eyes were glued to the door. "We're supposed to meet here. He wants to talk to me about something."

The fact that she talked about him in present tense demonstrated that she thought he was alive. I didn't want to be the one who broke it to her that he wasn't. Being the bearer of bad news wasn't in my skill set. I preferred delivering happy news, like *I found your dog* or *You dropped ten dollars* or *Hey, your lawn is on fire.*

"Why can't I go in there?" the woman pressed.

"I think we should wait for the police," I said quickly.

"Why?" She turned fearful eyes back to the door.

"Because we don't want to contaminate the crime scene," I answered.

Edna didn't respond, but her face grew pale. For a few moments we stood there in silence. I was worried she was going to demand to know what was happening, but she didn't. From the look on her face, I was fairly certain she didn't really want to know.

Rex arrived at the same time as the ambulance. I nodded toward the door, and he gave me a look that said *I knew you couldn't go one month without a dead body in your wake.* He came back out a moment later, shoving his cell into his pocket.

"This is Edna Lou Murphy," I said quickly before he could speak. "The woman I told you about. She's supposed to meet her cousin Ike here." I wiggled my eyebrows to clue him in.

"Ms. Murphy"—Rex shook her hand—"I'm Detective Ferguson. Can you describe your cousin? Ike, was it?"

The elderly woman nodded. "That's right. Ike Murphy. Well, he's old. Skinny and old, like me."

Rex led us to a park bench as Dr. Soo Jin Body—the town coroner—pulled up.

"Will someone tell me what is going on?" Edna watched as the beautiful medical examiner walked into the cabin and shut the door.

Rex put his hand on her back. "I'm sorry to tell you this, but I think your cousin has been murdered."

Edna's mouth opened and closed three times without speaking. Then she laughed.

"This is a prank! Ike always was a prankster." She smiled at me.

Her smile faded when I slowly shook my head.

"I'm so sorry, Edna Lou. I found his body inside. He's gone."

"That can't be true. I just saw him at the gas station an hour ago. He was fit as a fiddle."

I didn't tell her that "fit as a fiddle" didn't often include an axe in your head.

"Ms. Wrath…" Rex looked at me. "Could you excuse us for a moment?"

I got up and walked away. As unhappy as I was that he was kicking me out of this case, I couldn't argue with him in front of the old lady who'd just lost her cousin. I wandered over to the merry-go-round and sat down.

Officer Kevin Dooley arrived in a squad car. He was wrist deep in a bag of little donuts and had powdered sugar all over his uniform. Yeesh. Kevin and I went all the way back to our childhood. He was a mouth breather then and was a mouth breather now. The only difference was that he didn't eat paste anymore, and for reasons I've never been able to understand, now had a gun.

From a short distance away, I could hear Rex mumbling softly to Edna, who stared at him as if he were a lowland gorilla who spoke perfect French. She wasn't crying or screaming. She looked kind of like she didn't believe him.

This was murder. Axe murder. Like what happened to Mehitable over a century ago. It certainly couldn't be the same murderer. The killer would have to be more than one hundred years old. No, that made no sense. A centenarian wouldn't be able to hold an axe, let alone raise it above his head.

It was possible that the murder wasn't even connected to the past. But then again, it took place in the local historical society's vintage log cabin, so my thoughts ran to it being connected.

I pictured the layout in my mind. It had been dark when I'd entered. The killer probably had the lights out, or Ike didn't know where the switch was, and waited in darkness. Was it possible the killer was after something in the cabin?

Or someone?

My eyes snapped back to Edna Lou. Was she the target? I hoped not. I really liked her.

The park had filled up with people who'd seen the emergency vehicles and showed up to see what happened. It was a small town where most people knew everyone. How many of these people knew Ike and Edna?

I didn't recognize many faces—just a few from the businesses nearby.

It had surprised me when Edna mentioned my grandmother. Wrath was not a common name, but no one I'd met here ever asked about my connection. Maybe that was because Rex and Dr. Body were new here, so they thought I was too.

Kelly and Kevin knew who I was. At least, I thought Kevin did. You never knew what was going through that brain.

My thoughts drifted back to Adelaide Wrath. When it came to my family history, on both sides, she was the only ancestor I knew. That seemed like a shame. I didn't know Dad's parents or Mom's father because they'd all passed away before I was born.

Why didn't I ask more questions about family history? Mehitable's face popped into my head, and I pulled the photo of normal Mimi, that I'd printed from the microfiche, out of my pocket. She really did look like me. Or…I looked like her.

I snapped a picture of the photo on my cell and sent it to Mom and Dad with a question mark.

"Ms. Wrath?" Rex loomed over me. He always used my surname when he was working, even though everyone knew we were engaged. "Would you take Ms. Murphy home?"

Edna Lou was still sitting on the bench, staring blindly into the distance. She looked like she was in shock.

I nodded. "Of course."

Edna got up and followed me to my car. She didn't mention her own vehicle, and I didn't ask because, frankly, she wasn't in any shape to drive.

"We can come back later and get your car, if you want," I said.

The woman stared at me for a moment before giving me her address.

She lived two blocks away. So much for dealing with her car. This woman had walked here.

Once inside, I left her on the couch and went to find some tea. She had a kettle on the stove, but I thought she needed it quickly, so I heated the water in the microwave and dropped the tea bag into it. Hopefully, she wouldn't notice.

"Do you want any sugar or cream?" I shouted from the kitchen.

"No" was all she said.

Back in the living room, I set the cup on the coffee table and sat beside her. She looked different. Frail. And stoic. Not a single tear fell. That wasn't unusual. People were usually in shock first and then cried later.

"I'm so sorry about Ike." I patted her hand.

When she didn't respond, I looked up. The walls were covered with portraits from years gone by. Were these members of her family, or had Edna Lou brought her work home with her?

"Those people didn't have homes," the woman said at last.

I couldn't take my eyes off the rows and rows of serious faces from the past. "What do you mean?"

She shook her head, as if to clear it. "Those people all lived here, in Who's There, at one time or another. Most of these didn't have any family. I found a whole file folder full of unwanted photos. I felt sorry for them, so I brought them here and framed them."

It was kind of spooky. No one smiled in these photos. They were obviously staged, and the folks looked awkward. I felt a little pang of guilt that I hadn't learned more about my family's past.

As I walked through the room, I passed hundreds of old pictures, all from the nineteenth and early twentieth centuries. In a way, it was pretty cool, seeing the clothes and hairstyles. I wondered what they were thinking.

Pets were in a few pictures. I thought of Philby, hair slicked to one side, scowling in a black and white background.

And then I saw it. A large print of what had to be the Peters family. I'd never seen one of Theobald and Euphemia in their later years. He was a large, burly man with a friendly smile and giant eyebrows. She was short, heavyset, and looked like she'd spent the day sucking on lemons. Their daughter, Mimi and Eustace's mother, had been dead for a long time and was absent.

Eustace stood behind his grandfather, his hand awkwardly placed on his granddad's shoulder. A teenaged Mehitable stood behind Euphemia, her hand on her grandmother's shoulder. None of them smiled. It looked like they were in a studio because the background seemed to be painted.

The frame was very old—silver that was completely tarnished. Was it original to the picture? My eyes drifted back to Mimi. This would've been maybe ten years before she lost her mind. What had she been thinking when the photographer took the picture?

I was pretty sure it wasn't *wubble*.

# CHAPTER SIX

———

"Edna?" I had a thought. "In your files at the Historical Society, do you have information on who owned what land over the years?"

The woman came out of her quiet little coma and thought about this. "I have the original plat maps. And I have some records of how the town grew. Is that what you mean?"

I nodded. "I was just wondering who owned my house, or the land, before I did. I thought it might be a fun project for the girls in my troop—to find the histories of their houses."

Mostly, I just wanted to find another piece of the puzzle and find out why the map had been buried in my Salute to Scotland garden.

The woman stared at me for a moment, as if torn between grief for Ike and something useful to do. "Yes, I should have some of those records. We can find more at the library or county courthouse, if we need to."

Perfect.

"I'll set up a day when my troop can come by." Of course, that would have to be after the police were done with the murder site.

"That would be nice." Edna Lou nodded. "It might be a good distraction from…from…" She struggled with the words. "What's your address?"

I told her and then pointed it out in the map in the back of the phone book.

She squinted. "Ah, yes. The town expanded in the 1950s. Your house was part of that."

"That would make sense. My house was built in 1952."

"I'm not entirely sure," Edna said slowly. "But I think that was part of Eustace Peters' farm." She nodded. "Yes, I'm sure of it. But I'd better check to make sure."

Eustace's farm? That couldn't be right. According to the lore, he spent a few years looking for the treasure. How did the map end up buried on his land if he hadn't solved that problem?

"If you don't mind, I need some time alone," Edna said.

"Oh! Sorry! I should go. When would you like me to bring the girls by?"

"How about the day after tomorrow?" she asked, rubbing her eyes.

I nodded. "I'll set it up." As I started for the door, I turned to her. "Again, I'm so sorry about your cousin Ike."

Edna nodded but waved me off. Just before I left, I snapped a picture of the Peters family photo.


I was driving the two blocks back by the park when I saw that Dr. Body and the ambulance were still at the cabin, which was surrounded by crime scene tape. It couldn't hurt to stop by.

Dr. Soo Jin Body was our coroner and medical examiner, rolled into one. The beautiful Korean-American doctor had been a little bit of a thorn in my side. Now she counted herself as one of my friends. She also owned Bond and Moneypenny—Philby's two other kittens. My former CIA handler, Riley, had given them to her in an unusual moment where he was the one dazzled by her.

As I got out of the car, I figured out a way to get info without looking like I was fishing for intel. That was the number one thing about being a spy—extracting information while seeming to do something else entirely. That, and Frisbee golf. Spies really like Frisbee golf.

"Soo Jin!" I waved as I walked toward her.

The doctor smiled, and the heavens opened, birds sang, and the world was at peace. I'm not kidding—she was that beautiful.

"Hi, Merry! What are you doing here?"

"I found the body and took the victim's cousin home."

"Ah." She shoved her perfectly sleek bob behind one ear. "That explains it."

"I was driving past and saw you. I've been meaning to ask you something."

"Sure! What is it?"

*Prepare to be disarmed, Soo Jin.* "Would you be a bridesmaid in my wedding in December?"

To tell you the truth, I should've thought of her before. I didn't really have many options outside of Kelly and twelve little girls who'd all decided they were my flower girls. Soo Jin had helped out with a number of troop events. It was time to call her friend.

"Oh! Merry!"

The woman threw herself into my arms. That would've been nice if she hadn't been wearing white coveralls with red specks. But I wasn't squeamish.

"Yes! Of course I will!" She pulled back, looking even more radiant.

I'd heard that no one was supposed to upstage the bride on her wedding day, but that just went out the window. Dr. Body would look amazing in a burlap sack. Fortunately, I was above vanity.

"Yeah? Great!" I smiled and then realized I genuinely meant it.

Soo Jin looked down at her coveralls, just now realizing what she was wearing. "I'm sorry! I guess I got excited."

I shrugged. "Don't worry about it. Kelly is the matron of honor—whatever that is. And the troop are all flower girls."

Soo Jin laughed. It sounded like soothing wind chimes that made me feel relaxed and sleepy. "Twelve flower girls!"

"Actually," I said, "Kelly and I are taking them to pick out dresses tomorrow if you want to join us. I haven't decided on the bridemaids' dresses yet."

That was technically true. I explained that my colors were green and white, and I had ordered my dress, but still hadn't done anything on other dresses.

"Green and white?" Soo Jin's right eyebrow arched. "Girl Scout colors?"

I nodded. "I didn't realize that when I picked them. That won't be a problem, will it?"

"I love it!"

Of course she did. She'd look good in green, taupe, blaze orange or puce—whatever color *that* was.

"Meet us at A Storybook Tale, downtown at ten, if you can swing it."

"I promise," she said.

Adopting a casual air of what I hoped appeared to be indifference, I waved my hand at the cabin. "This is terrible. Poor Ike." Okay, I didn't really know Ike Murphy, but she didn't need to know that.

"You said you found him?" Soo Jin asked.

I told her the whole story.

"It's definitely murder," Soo Jin said. "From what I've seen here, there was a trajectory that the weapon took. He'd been near the back wall, on the other side of the table, when someone in the doorway threw the axe at him. Death was caused by trauma to the skull."

My jaw dropped. "Someone threw the axe?"

Axes were big with long handles. I'd heard of hatchet throwing, but not an axe.

"Are you sure it was thrown?"

Soo Jin shrugged. "If it was, whoever did this had excellent aim." She stepped forward, holding a pen in her hand like it was a tiny, micro-scaled axe.

I thought about this for a moment.

"It was dark in the cabin when I went in. The shades had been pulled down. The murderer had good night vision."

"Or," Dr. Body added, "he knew exactly where the victim would be."

We stared in silence at the cabin. Pulling off this murder was an amazing accomplishment. It wasn't going to get the killer a trophy or anything. Still, it was impressive.

"So…" Soo Jin wriggled out of her coveralls.

A jogger passing by was staring at her and tripped over a stick. He righted himself and kept running.

"Tomorrow at ten." She hadn't even noticed.

"Tomorrow at ten," I agreed.

\*   \*   \*

"What are you doing?"

Rex's voice startled me, and the hatchet I'd been throwing at the big tree in my backyard bounced harmlessly off a branch and embedded itself in the ground near a very worried squirrel.

"Um, I heard that there's a Buckskinners' Rendezvous coming up. I'm practicing."

"A Buckskinners' Rendezvous that happens to have the same setup as the murder scene from today?" Rex pointed to the table between me and the tree, the duct tape wall cutout around me, and the dummy made to look like Ike Murphy and leaning against the tree. It wasn't a very good likeness. To be fair, it would have been hard to do that since his face was missing.

"Yes," I said.

Rex ran his hands through his short black hair. He was so adorable when he did that, because it gave him a slight vulnerable appearance that made me love him even more.

"Merry, what are you doing?"

I took a huge leap of faith. "I think this murder is related to Mehitable's murder."

My fiancé stared at me. "You're serious?"

"Absolutely." Frankly, I had no idea if it was linked, but that sounded good.

He tried another tactic. "How did you know about the Buckskinners' Rendezvous?"

My turn to look stunned.

He had me and knew it. "The Buckskinners are in the state park, setting up for the annual event."

My mind raced frantically as I tried to come up with a plausible lie.

"You had no idea, did you?"

"Do you think one of the reenactors killed Ike…" I mused aloud.

He sighed, went to one of the lawn chairs, and sat down. That was when I noticed he had two bottles of beer. I took one and joined him. Normally I was a wine girl. But occasionally I could be found with beer. Philby and Martini trotted over to him, and after a heavy petting session (of the cats), they sat at our feet.

"Merry," he said cautiously, "tell me you aren't investigating this."

I clutched my chest, ignoring the damning evidence in my backyard. "Me? No. Why would you think that?"

"Because Dr. Body told me you were lurking in the park after I'd gone."

"I wasn't lurking. I was asking her to be one of my bridemaids, oh suspicious one."

Rex's right eyebrow went up. "She said that too. So, I invited her over for dinner."

My jaw dropped for the second time today. "You did what?"

"Hello?" Soo Jin shouted from the side of the house. She came through the gate, a bucket of fried chicken in one arm, Bond and Moneypenny in the other.

The kittens squirmed out of her grip as Philby and Martini snapped to attention. Martini made a mad dash for her siblings, and they collided into a three-way feline pileup, to the sound of three coconuts smacking together. The three cats collapsed, unconscious.

Philby trotted over to where her kittens lay, then looked at me as if to say this was all my fault.

"Are they alright?" Soo Jin stared in horror.

"Oh yeah." I got up and pulled the table over to the lawn chairs. "They're fine."

Soo Jin handed me the chicken before running back to her car and returning with three side dishes and a bottle of white wine. Now she was talking. I'd have had to kick her out if she'd just brought chicken. I had to maintain my standards, after all.

While we ate, the cats all came to. Philby watched as the three kittens played with each other, each playing the role of vicious cougar. Every now and then, she'd swat one. That was the extent of her exercise and mommy time.

"Thanks for dinner," I said to Soo Jin when we'd finished.

You probably thought we chatted, exchanging pithy dialogue while we ate. But when it comes to fried chicken, and a dinner I didn't have to prepare or order, I was engaged in the business of eating. Why Rex and Soo Jin didn't talk was beyond me.

"I'm so excited about being in the wedding!" Soo Jin said. "Thank you so much for inviting me to be your bridemaid!"

"No problem," I said, while my brain finally realized what I'd done and made a sound that sounded like *ayooooogah.*

"Are you just having two?" Soo Jin asked. "Besides all those flower girls, that is."

I nodded and looked at my fiancé. "Rex, who are you going to ask?"

He'd better not say Kevin Dooley.

"I'm thinking about that," Rex said and said no more. "Do you think Kelly's husband would do it?"

I shrugged. "I don't see why not. You and Robert get along well. Who else? You need two."

"I'll think of something." He reached for his beer. "Don't worry."

*And I'll be investigating Ike's murder*, I thought to myself as I buttered my fifth biscuit.

# CHAPTER SEVEN

———

If you've ever wondered what the most annoying sound in the world was, I had the answer. It was twelve little girls squealing as they looked at flower girl dresses. Kelly and the girls seemed to arrive en masse, and they swarmed the store before I could lay down some ground rules. Like no touching anything. No squealing. No fire accelerants…the usual stuff.

"Ladies!" Kelly held up the Girl Scout quiet sign, and the girls calmed down. "Let's sit in a semicircle, please."

We were in the room with a small stage and a three-way mirror. To keep the girls from tearing the store apart, we'd decided to have them sit down and one of them would model dresses. As we explained this, the room erupted.

It turned out, to nobody's surprise, that every single girl wanted to be the model. As tomboyish as my troop was, they still loved girly stuff. Right now, the arguing could probably be heard in Des Moines.

Soo Jin walked into the room, and the girls didn't even notice her. Wow. They always swarmed the doctor whenever they saw her. She gave me a shrug.

"They all want to be the model," I explained and added how we thought it would be good to have one girl try on the dresses.

Dr. Body clapped her hands loudly, and the girls turned to stare at her.

"I've got an idea!" She walked over to a notepad and tore off several pages. "Each one of you will nominate one girl to be the model." Kelly grabbed pencils off the counter and handed them out.

"Will this work?" I whispered to Kelly when she rejoined me.

"It might," my co-leader said unconvincingly.

After a few moments of glorious silence, Soo Jin collected the pieces of paper and the three of us began to count.

It didn't go well. Either every single girl voted for a different girl each, or they all voted for themselves.

"Now what?" Kelly mumbled.

I turned around and smiled. "The votes are in! Inez, you will be our model."

My best friend hissed, "You lied to them."

I nodded. "Yes, but they don't know that."

As Inez was led away by Zelda, the store's one and I think only employee, the girls eyed each other suspiciously. Clearly, they knew that nobody but Inez voted for Inez, but they had no proof since I pocketed all of the ballots.

"I'm not sure that was a good idea," Kelly mumbled.

Here I'd thought I was being clever. "It worked, didn't it?"

She couldn't disagree with me.

I pointed in the direction of the dressing rooms, "Where's Betsy? She helped us before."

Kelly shrugged. "Zelda said she quit."

"When did you talk to her?" And why hadn't I noticed we had a different woman helping us? My brain wasn't what it used to be.

"When I made the appointment to come in. Now focus."

After a few moments, the excitement picked up again as the girls eagerly awaited the first dress. Soo Jin sat in the middle of them, and they peppered her with questions about what kind of shoes they might get.

I was still amazed that the parents were down with this. When Kelly and I told them we wanted all the girls to participate, they were very enthusiastic. Each set of parents agreed to cough up the money once the dress was selected. That was touching. And a relief. Hell hath no fury like a little girl scorned.

Inez strutted into the room like an adult supermodel on a catwalk. The first dress was white with lots of lace and a huge green bow sash around the middle. She climbed up on the pedestal to a loud, collective gasp. The girls started to get up, but we made them sit back down.

"It's a pretty dress," I said to Kelly.

"That one!" several girls shouted.

"Wait!" Kelly said. "There are more. Just wait until we're done."

This seemed to make them even crazier as they squealed in anticipation.

"What if they can't all decide on one dress?" I asked.

Inez retreated to the dressing room, and Zelda came back out and hung the dress up, facing out to display it.

"They have to agree," Kelly said, as if she really thought it would be that easy.

"By the way," I said, "can the girls all meet us at the Historical Society tomorrow afternoon?"

I filled my co-leader in on the idea of the girls investigating the history of their houses.

"I think so. Did you show Edna the map?"

I shook my head. "I did put it into a plastic sleeve."

A loud scream erupted as Inez trotted out in a green dress with white trim. It kind of looked like a birthday cake. Or maybe I was just obsessed with cake. She stood on the pedestal and turned around slowly. This dress went all the way to the floor and had a poufy skirt.

The noise was deafening.

"Does that mean they like this one better?" I asked.

Kelly shrugged. "I just want to know how they had green and white dresses. We haven't even picked mine out yet."

"About that…" I said. "I asked Soo Jin to be a bridemaid. That'll work, right?

My best friend threw her arms around me. "Well done! I think that's a great idea!"

Oh good. She liked it.

"Has Rex decided on groomsmen?"

I shook my head. "I think he's leaning toward Robert."

"What if he picks Riley?"

I turned very slowly to look at her. "Riley? You can't be serious."

Riley was my former CIA handler and former boyfriend. He worked for the FBI now, and was still sending me some pretty strong signals that he wasn't over me. Rex had to know, although he was too much of a gentleman to say anything.

Kelly should've known better, but she pressed the issue. "Why not? He's Finn's godfather, and you've known him forever."

"Not gonna happen. It would be too weird. And speaking of weird, why is it so hard for Rex to find groomsmen?"

My best friend put her hand on my arm. "Is that bothering you?"

"A little." I had to admit, it did.

Inez had left the room, and the girls were back to talking to Soo Jin about floral headbands.

Kelly shook her head. "Not all men have a pack of friends they do everything with. Robert has a couple of friends from work, but mostly we just hang out together."

"I guess…" I had to let this go. We had several months to go before the wedding and plenty of time for Rex to decide what he wanted to do.

"He could just have a best man," Kelly said. "There's no such thing as unconventional anymore. After all, you have twelve flower girls."

I nodded. "I think you and Soo Jin should look at dresses while we're here."

I barely finished my sentence before Kelly raced over, grabbed Soo Jin, and hit the racks. Huh. I guess she was really excited about this.

Inez came out wearing the third dress. It was a simple white slip dress, but she had a ring of white silk roses in her hair. A hush fell over the group. Did that mean they liked it? It wasn't as fancy as the others, but it was pretty.

In this, the girls were torn. Half declared their love for the dress and the other half disagreed. Inez looked a little miffed as she stormed back into the dressing room. I took Soo Jin's place with the girls.

"What do you think so far?" I asked as the girls crowded around.

"I'm waiting to see all of them," Caterina said. Most of the others seemed to agree.

"I like the first dress!" one of the Kaitlyns said, and the others nodded.

"I liked the second one," Lauren interjected, and the two Hannahs agreed with her.

This wasn't going to be easy. I decided to change the subject.

"Are you guys free tomorrow? I've got a little investigative assignment for you."

The dresses were promptly forgotten.

"Is this about Mad Mimi's murder?" Betty asked.

"Yes," I said. "But we're going to have to pretend it's about something else."

"I think we should wear disguises," Ava said.

"I'll bring brass knuckles," Betty added.

"No. We're going to the Historical Society in the park to research Who's There's history." I explained how each girl would look up their own address on the town plat and how we'd research it. And then I explained that we didn't need brass knuckles. Betty looked disappointed.

"I'm thinking most of the town was owned by the Peters family. Many of you probably live on those lots. It might give us some insight into the treasure."

A rousing cheer went up. It was decided.

Then, Inez entered the room.

The dress she wore was…um…bizarre. It looked like a pageant dress. Covered in green sequined flowers and marabou feathers, the gown had a mermaid skirt and faux skin-baring netting on the arms and midriff. Inez looked more like a Las Vegas show girl than a flower girl.

The girls rushed the podium, surrounding her with *oohs* and *ahs*. No! They couldn't love this dress!

The noise drew the attention of Kelly and Soo Jin, whose jaws dropped when they saw the monstrosity. It took them a moment to shoo the girls back to their seats on the floor.

Inez looked like a deranged peacock. On her head was one very long feather attached to a headband. Glitter and sequins blinded us when she spun around.

"That's it!" Emily screamed, and the girls quickly agreed.

Kelly drove Inez back into the dressing area and had a few quick words with the manager.

"What was that?" I asked when she returned.

"I don't know," Kelly answered. "But I told her to pick traditional dresses."

Soo Jin just shook her head without speaking. Apparently the sight of that horror show was too much for her. But if it looked good on anyone, it would be Dr. Body.

After the girls calmed down, Inez returned wearing a green velvet bodice with a high lace collar and white satin skirt. This was more like it. Zelda had even pinned a sprig of holly to the dress at the sash belt.

The girls were unimpressed. They'd seen the holy grail and had no interest in any substitutions. The rest of the morning passed with one beautiful dress after another, but not one touched the enthusiasm for the Vegas show-girl dress.

When she was finished, Inez joined the girls. Kelly and Soo Jin helped Zelda carry out and display all of the dresses…except for one.

"What about the peacock dress?" Lauren demanded.

They *named* it. In my experience with them, that was a bad sign. Once a horse, or spider, or canoe was named, there was no going back because that was the hands-down favorite horse, or spider, or canoe.

"That's the one we want!" Emily and Ava shouted.

The rest of the girls agreed.

"That dress is way too expensive," Kelly lied. "I don't think your parents would want to pay for it."

I nodded in agreement but felt that the die had been cast.

"Mommy said any dress I wanted," Inez sniffed, and the others agreed.

"I'm not sure they can make twelve dresses before December, what with all that detailed work," Soo Jin attempted.

They glared at her so hard she burst into flame.

Okay, she didn't. But if they could have, they would have. And to be honest, having a troop of Girl Scouts with exploding laser vision would be cool.

We were now faced with an epic dilemma. The girls had picked the ugliest dress imaginable. And they were holding firm. No one was more stubborn than my troop when they wanted something. And they wanted this dress.

After thirty minutes of shrewd negotiations that would exhaust the Israelis and Palestinians, the girls relented on one condition. They agreed to pick a second choice, and we agreed to let their parents decide.

Emily had taken pictures of all of the dresses. She uploaded them and made a snapshot of the dresses together with their prices. The strange (but good) thing was, they picked the green velvet and white satin dress as second. The bad thing was, even with all the sequins, beads, and feathers, the ugly dress was a tiny bit cheaper.

She sent the image to each girl, and after making sure they would be at the park the next day at one o'clock, we waited with them as they got into their parents' cars. It was all on the adults now.

"I'm so sorry." Zelda wrung her hands. "That dress wasn't for them. It was for a beauty pageant. Inez saw it and demanded to try it on. I had no idea they'd like it."

"It's okay." I sighed. "Now let's look at dresses for these two."

Kelly and Soo Jin narrowed down their choices to two dresses. One was green velvet, like the flower girl dresses, and the other one was a simple green satin with white trim. I left the decision to them, and they were measured. By the time the whole venture was over (the green velvet won out), it was midafternoon and I was starving. I suggested a late lunch.

"I can't," Soo Jin said. "I have to get back to the hospital."

"Me too," Kelly said. "My shift starts in half an hour."

We said our goodbyes, and I made my way to Oleo's—the best burger place in town. I didn't mind eating alone. Besides, it would give me a little time to think.

The waitress took my order and dropped off an iced tea. I pulled Mehitable's diary out of my purse and started to read.

It wasn't half bad. A little dull in some places, but interesting in others. Whenever she mentioned Eustace, it was obvious that she'd loved him and her grandparents. She'd had the usual education that any other girl had—which meant that she'd gone to a one-room schoolhouse. Once she'd hit her teenage years, she'd begun writing more. This was normal, teenage stuff, not the weird junk kids have now, like hashtags and anime. What was up with anime?

The interesting parts of the diary start when she hits twenty-five, one year before she lost her mind.

*February 30*

*Dearest Friend, Eustace is gone, and I have no one to talk to. I understand that he is busy now with his business and new family. But I miss him. Grandpapa has been very quiet of late. Grandmama is pushing me to find a suitor, but I'd rather stay here with Tinkles. She has told me that they are leaving their fortune to me. I am not quite certain what that means. And I am unsure that I like the idea. Tinkles has told me that he agrees.*

February 30? Unless I'd crossed over into another dimension, there was no February 30. Maybe Mehitable had started losing her mind early. I could understand that. I felt like I was losing my mind a little more every day. And what was that about Tinkles the llama talking to her?

*March 3*

*Dearest Friend, today I churned butter. All day. I like butter. Butter is my favorite.*

Some days, her posts were better than others.

*March 15*

*Dearest Friend, Tinkles has run away! I have searched the whole town and cannot find him!*

How do you lose something as big as a llama? The waitress dropped off my burger and shake. I did something I never did—put off eating. The diary did not need my sticky fingerprints all over it. Besides, it was just getting good.

*March 16*

*Dearest Friend, Tinkles has been found! She was in the new park, chewing on that little log cabin. I will have to take care not to lose him again. We had a long talk and made a deal—he can chew on things outside of the house, and I won't say anything to get him in trouble. Also, I am to make him a hat. He likes hats.*

I think I should admit that I sighed a sigh of relief. I didn't know what I'd do if Philby or Martini were missing. And cats were a lot harder to find than a giant llama. My hunger got the best of me, and I set the diary aside to eat.

Halfway through my burger, I looked to see if there was a text from Mom regarding the photo. It was a little weird that she hadn't gotten back to me. But then, the life of a senator's wife was insanely busy. I decided to give her more time.

Edna Lou had said she thought my property was part of Eustace's farm originally. We'd have to confirm that tomorrow with the Historical Society records, but if that was true, that might explain how the map ended up in my yard.

But then again…if Eustace couldn't find the treasure, why would the map have been in his possession? Could Mehitable have buried the map on her brother's farm in hopes he'd find the gold? Or had he found the map, and after searching and turning up nothing, did he bury it himself just to get rid of it?

If I were him, I'd hold on to the map in hopes of someday locating the money. Even if I was completely frustrated, I didn't think I'd bury it in a box in the ground. I'd probably just put it in a file in my desk.

It was possible that he didn't do that because he didn't want his heirs going crazy trying to find the treasure. Or he was just angry and acting illogically. If his sister Mimi had buried it on her brother's land, she could've been trying to help him out, in her own bizarre way.

Then again, the woman was stark-raving mad. She could've done it for any of thousands of reasons that made sense only to her.

The diary had to have some sort of clue. Granted, it ended when she went crazy. And she died years later. Still, there must be something personal about her in it. Something that mentioned a special place where she used to go. Or a peek into her personality that could explain why she went crazy.

I paid my bill, and once I got home, I spent the rest of the day reading the diary, from front to back, taking notes as I went. There were a lot of stories of everyday chores, which made it kind of fun to read, especially if you were *really* into butter.

Mimi never explained, but I got the impression that her grandparents weren't into hiring servants to help around the house. Mimi must have picked up the slack. And wrote endlessly about it. There were ten whole pages dedicated to embroidering a llama on handkerchiefs. She didn't mention making hats for Tinkles. I wondered how he felt about that. After all, a deal was a deal.

At some point, I called Edna to confirm our meeting tomorrow with the troop. Then I ordered pizza and invited Rex over for dinner. I needed to know if we could even use the cabin, and I was curious about Ike Murphy.

"Pizza?" Rex said as he walked in the door. "You spoil me."

I agreed. "I really do. You don't deserve me."

As we ate, I told him about the flower girl fiasco and that my bridemaids had selected their dress. In order to get the intel from him regarding the murder from earlier, I'd need to start it off by talking about his favorite subject...the wedding.

He pushed aside his empty plate and poured us each another glass of wine. "I'm going to ask Robert to stand up for me."

I nodded. "That's good news. Are you going to have another groomsman?"

Rex sighed. "I would be happy with only one."

"That's not how this works," I pointed out. "There are rules. You told me you wanted a traditional wedding. I have two bridemaids, so you need another groomsman."

Rex ran his hands through his short black hair. "It's not that easy. I can't ask the guys at work, because I don't want them to feel pressured. And I don't have a group of men I hang out with, because I hang out with you."

Riley popped into my mind. I popped him back out.

"What about your father?"

Rex had been estranged from his parents for some time. I'd only recently brought them back together. And I liked his dad. Mike Ferguson was a large, loud man with a happy demeanor.

Rex reached for another slice. "I don't know about that. I mean, who has their dad in their wedding party?"

I shrugged, letting him off the hook. "Okay. One will do."

My fiancé leaned forward and kissed me. He was happy. Now to more interesting subjects.

"Is the cabin still a crime scene? When I took Edna Lou home, I suggested bringing the troop back tomorrow to work on a historical project."

His eyebrows went up. "Really?"

"Of course. I asked her if she knew the history of my property, and she said she thought it was part of Eustace's farm originally."

That got his attention. "You know, that might explain why the map was on your property."

"Then she suggested I bring the girls in to research the history of their homes. It's a great idea. I'm sure I can find a badge or something to fit that."

He nodded. "That does sound like a fun idea. And educational."

"The only problem would be if the cabin is still roped off as a crime scene," I ventured.

Rex thought about this. "I think we wrapped the investigation. The forensics team from Des Moines was able to come down today and collect evidence. But…"

"What?"

"It's not clean. By that, I mean that it's a mess from the investigation."

I shrugged. "I'll clean it up in the morning."

"It's a big job."

"I can handle it." Time to bring the subject around to murder. "Ike Murphy was murdered, right?"

He sighed. "Yes. Definitely murdered. And we have the weapon. An axe."

"Any idea why?"

"Merry…"

"I thought we were going to work together on solving Mehitable Peters' murder. What if they're linked?"

He rubbed his eyes. "I'm not sure how they can be linked, since they died more than one hundred years apart.

Suspects from Mimi's murder would be dead by now. Even Edna Lou and her cousin are too young to have lived during that era."

"Come on! Two axe murders." Okay, so I was reaching with that one. "It makes sense that they are linked."

Rex didn't answer.

I tried something else. "I knew a lot of Murphys growing up. But Ike is much older than me. I had no idea he existed."

Rex looked at me for one long moment. "Okay, you're probably going to find out anyway. Ike Murphy lived in Who's There all of his life. For the last ten years, he's been a crossing guard and vice president of the Historical Society. He didn't have many friends, besides his cousin Edna Lou. And she's our prime suspect."

"Are you sure?" I was skeptical. "She can't even hold an axe, let alone swing or fling it. And what's her motive?"

"She knew the layout of that room better than anyone," Rex said. "She could've easily ambushed him. And there's the matter of the presidency of the Historical Society. Apparently he was gunning for her job."

I narrowed my eyes. "You're saying that she killed her cousin because he wanted her job? A job that's a volunteer position?"

"Anything is possible. Look, in my professional career, all but two years have been spent in other police departments. I've seen family members murder each other for much less. Once, a man killed his brother because he cut his grilled cheese sandwich diagonally instead of in rectangles."

I was unconvinced.

"It's no secret that Edna Lou loved her position, even if it was voluntary. I talked to people in the mayor's office today, and they said she was obsessed with it. This is her whole life. And when someone threatens that, you're capable of anything."

I thought back to the dozens of framed pictures of people she wasn't even related to that filled the walls in her house. Rex definitely had a point. I didn't even have framed pictures of my parents…and I loved them.

"Okay," I reasoned. "I'll watch her tomorrow and see how she reacts to things. Maybe I can find something new out."

He sighed. "I'll call the station right now and have someone go down there to remove the crime tape and drop off the keys. I don't like the idea of you cleaning up the crime scene, but if you're determined…"

"I am." Okay, so I wasn't, really. I had no idea how to clean up a crime scene, but it would give me an exclusive look at the cabin.

"And don't worry about me." I smiled. "I know just the person to help me. Someone who knows how to clean just about anything."

# CHAPTER EIGHT

———

Kelly wiped her forehead with her arm. "I can't believe I let you talk me into this."

A bucket of dirty water sat at her feet, and she was holding a sponge. An hour into it and we were already tired. And it was hot. July had finally woke up and gone, "Whoa! People are comfortable? What?"

"You're the only person I know who knows how to do this," I said as I wiped off a display of brochures. "And it's your troop too. You were the only choice."

This wasn't totally accurate. I could've asked Dr. Body. She was a coroner and worked around this kind of thing all the time. But I wasn't ready for that step in our relationship. Oddly, cleaning up this crime scene seemed too intimate.

"I'm not at work." Kelly said.

"Well…" I looked dubiously at a pamphlet on agricultural technology in the 1960s, decided it was too far gone, and tossed it into the garbage bag I held. "Think of it as a service for your Girl Scout troop."

I was pretty sure she growled, but she said no more. We worked hard. The cabin had a very weak air-conditioning system, so by the time we walked outside, we were soaked with sweat. Twelve little girls and Edna Lou stared at us. They were early. And there we were, covered in sweat and grime.

The screams could be heard two counties away. I was still not sure it they were screams of joy or fear.

Kelly quickly disposed of the cleaning supplies as the girls peppered her with questions.

"Is that the crime scene?" Caterina's eyes grew wide.

Ava asked, "Who was murdered?"

"Did you do it?" Betty folded her arms across her chest.

"Is that why you cleaned it up?" one of the Kaitlyns asked, looking a little too eager for an answer.

"Was he a bad guy?" Hannah the First asked.

Emily rolled her eyes. "Of course he was, or Mrs. Wrath wouldn't have killed him!"

I left Kelly to respond to these questions and pulled Edna Lou aside. "Are you sure you want to do this today?"

She looked astonished. "Of course I want to do this today! I've never seen this much interest in local history! Besides…" She sniffed delicately. "Ike would want it that way."

The girls sat in the grass, and I addressed them.

"We are guests here, and we will be respectful. This is Ms. Murphy and she knows all about Who's There's history. You will not ask weird questions. You will ask questions relevant to today's activities."

"What's *relevant* mean?" one of the Kaitlyns asked.

Betty rolled her eyes. "It's a movie where Leo DiCaprio gets mauled by a bear and almost murdered."

"Ohhhh…" The gasp went up.

"It means," Kelly said, "related. Ask about things related to what we will be doing here today."

That was when Edna Lou, or Ms. Murphy to the girls, took over. She talked about the Historical Society and the cabin.

"This cabin was the first home to Theobald and Euphemia Peters, the founders of this town. They lived in it for six months before moving into the big Victorian house on Main Street. There's a taxidermist there *now*."

I felt a twinge of guilt for writing that check.

"Why did he build a cabin?" Lauren asked, violating the unspoken code of raising her hand first. "Why not just build the house first?"

Edna beamed. "That's an excellent question."

"Very revenant." Betty nodded.

I toyed with correcting her, but decided against it.

"When they moved here, they were the only family in this location. Theobald had promised men in Des Moines that he'd build a lumber mill here for them to work in. So the lumber mill was the first building, after the cabin and before the house."

"They also built a bar," Betty interrupted. "And a lot of people lost their hands in the lumber mill."

"Betty!" Kelly hissed.

"She's right," I said. "You can't fault her for doing their homework."

"Why did they lose their hands?" Ava asked.

Edna Lou looked conflicted.

"Working in a lumber mill is very dangerous. Lots of big saws," I said. "People weren't always careful."

It was true. Theobald Peters hadn't just built a lumber mill. He'd also built a tavern as an incentive for the workers to move here. Unfortunately, it had been open before the first shift of the day, and some of the inebriated workers had had accidents.

Euphemia had become adept at patching up injured workers and had changed the tavern's operating hours to start after the workday ended. Some believe she invented the first happy hour. Would Edna Lou add that tidbit to her goal of opening a historical museum here?

Edna Lou picked up as if this most recent conversation hadn't happened. "The cabin is the original, but the furniture was lost over the years. So we turned it into an office and sort of museum. Want to see inside?"

The girls were on their feet, but lined up politely, and they followed the elderly woman into the building. With the lights on and the blinds up, sun streamed into the little room. Edna Lou indicated where a bed would go and the location of the original fireplace. The girls listened with rapt attention.

"*I* didn't even know this stuff," Kelly whispered to me.

"You mean you weren't paying attention in Mrs. Walford's class in fourth grade?" I gasped with sarcasm.

She ignored me. "I can't believe two people lived in this one room. How did they manage?"

I shrugged. "Iowans lived in sod huts too. Can you imagine having earthworms crawling on your walls?"

She shot me a look. "I don't think I could've been a pioneer woman."

"You're joking. You of all people could handle it."

I wondered if they'd had cats. Images of Philby looking angry in the one window in the cabin—or looking angry to have to sit on a dirt floor—flooded my mind. At least back then she wouldn't have to suffer the fact that she looked like Hitler. He hadn't been around yet.

"The reason you're here today…" Edna Lou was speaking, and I elbowed Kelly. "Is to learn a little more about the town history by finding out the history of your houses. Does everyone know their address?"

I almost snorted. Of course they did. That had been one of our first meetings as a troop—learning personal safety measures by memorizing your address and phone number. The next meeting had been about defending yourself with sticks. I'd wanted to follow up with using cacti as a weapon, but Kelly had shot it down.

"Let's divide into three groups of four," Edna said, motioning to Kelly and me as she handed out copies of a blank map of the town. "You'll need to find your street and mark where your address is."

Edna took the four Kaitlyns. Kelly took the two Hannahs, Inez, and Caterina. Which left me with Ava, Emily, Lauren, and Betty.

The map was easy to follow. Every street was marked, so each girl easily figured out where their house was and drew a house on the map. Most of them were little boxes with a triangle for a roof. Betty's had a motorcycle, a bleeding stick figure, and five werewolves who looked like they were somewhat responsible for the stick figure's predicament.

Once all the addresses were accounted for, Edna Lou pulled a large map from one of the filing cabinets and taped it to a dry erase board. She handed each girl a little square magnet and asked her to place it on the map where her house was. Kelly and I were invited to do the same. When we were finished, fourteen little squares dotted the map.

"Well done!" Edna clapped her hands together. "And we are all over the map, which makes it interesting, doesn't it?"

The girls nodded sincerely. They were into this project. Which made me proud of them. I made a mental note to let the elementary school at the end of my block know about this. I thought other kids would like it too.

That, and there really weren't too many places to go for field trips in Who's There. We had a hospital and a small zoo. Occasionally kids could tour city hall or the police department, and one time there was a rather unfortunate trip to the sewage treatment plant that people still discussed in horrified, hushed tones, but that was rare. Now, they had the Historical Society too.

"Let's start here," Edna was saying as she pointed to the northwest corner of town.

There were two houses there, belonging to each of the two Hannahs.

"This corner development is the newest part of Who's There," she said. "Before that, the land had belonged to the government, with hopes of resettling the Ho-Chunk Indians here."

I did not know that.

"In the 1970s this land was developed into the houses you see today."

"Was there an Indian cemetery?" Lauren asked.

The other girls looked at the two Hannahs with envy in their eyes.

"No," Edna said, as if she heard this question every day. "The Ho-Chunk tribe wasn't interested in moving. It was just government land."

"Maybe it's Iowa's Roswell!" Inez said eagerly. "If it was owned by the government, maybe they buried aliens there!"

Edna Lou looked to me for help, but I just shrugged because I thought it was a fair question.

Kelly interjected, "If there'd been aliens buried there, the contractors would've found them when they dug the basements of those houses."

Hannah Number One piped up. "We don't have a basement."

Hannah the Second nodded eagerly. "We don't either!"

The girls squealed with delight, once again envious of the placement of the Hannahs' homes.

"Um…okay…" Edna said finally. "Next…" She pointed to the northeast corner of town, adjacent to the last area.

"This land had been originally owned by the railroad, which you know, runs past it. In 1939, the railroad decided to sell. They sold to farmers who'd lost their farms in the Great Depression and had to move into town."

"The Great Depression?" more than one girl asked.

"It was a time"—I gave an overly simplified explanation—"when a lot of people lost money and were poor."

"They lost their money? Like Mehit…Meh…Mimi?" Ava asked.

One of the Kaitlyns spoke up. "Did they hide it and make a treasure map?"

"Why couldn't they find their money?" added another Kaitlyn.

Edna smiled. She was getting the hang of my troop's quirkiness. "There's no treasure map or buried treasure. That's just an old legend."

"Yuh hunh!" Betty shouted and pointed at me. "We found the treasure map at Mrs. Wrath's!"

Did Betty just rat me out on the map?

Edna's eyes turned to me. I thought I detected a bit of excitement and hope in them. You could tell a lot about a person from their eyes. And it wasn't really their eyeballs I was talking about. It was the little wrinkling of skin around them. That was where the story came from.

"Did I hear right? You found a map to Mehitable Peters' treasure?"

I laughed and waved her off. "No, the girls are just confused."

I tried to use my mind to tell the girls to be quiet and hoped they were listening.

"We found *a* map, but I'm sure it wasn't *the* map." Technically this was true. There wasn't anything on the map that said it belonged to Mad Mimi or had anything to do with hidden treasure. Although, I was pretty sure it was hers.

Edna came out of her stupor. "I'd love to see it. To rule it out, of course."

"Does that mean," Emily asked, "that Mrs. Wrath lives on important land?"

Twelve faces swung back to the old woman.

Edna Lou looked at the map. I lived in the southwest corner of town. "That part of town was developed in the 1950s. It had originally been part of Eustace Peters' farm. When the family died off, the land was sold."

She said the words as if in a trance. I understood that. This woman had devoted her life to the town's history. Mehitable's Map would be like finding the fountain of youth, or Jimmy Hoffa. But I didn't want to show her the map. Not yet anyway.

"I'll bring it by," I said vaguely.

The woman brightened and seemed to remember where she was and what she was doing.

"Which leaves the southeast corner," she said. This was where all of the Kaitlyns lived. "This was the very first developed area, after the downtown area, that is. When the downtown area grew too large, they started building in this direction."

"Why not work their way out like a spiral?" Inez, future urban planner, asked.

"That would make sense, wouldn't it?" Edna nodded. "But the land on three sides belonged to the government, the railroad, and Eustace Peters. Land in the southeast was open. That's when we had a wave of Irish immigrants move here."

Edna Lou launched into a history of Irish immigration, and Kelly pulled me over to the side.

"Are you going to show her the map?"

"Not until I have to," I whispered. "I think we'd better make a copy of the map before we share it with anyone else."

Kelly looked toward the girls. "Good idea."

That was when I noticed that the room had gone quiet. I turned to look and saw that the girls and Edna were all staring at something in the corner on the floor. The corner where Ike's body was found. Had we missed something?

I pushed past everyone and looked in the direction they'd been staring. Something shiny was sticking out from under one of the cabinets. Getting down on my hands and knees, I reached under and pulled out a gold bar.

Now, how did that get there?

# CHAPTER NINE

―――――

"Mehitable's treasure!" Lauren gasped.

The other girls nodded. Edna Lou's eyes grew round, and the hair on my arms started to rise as I wrapped a piece of cloth around it in a vain hope of protecting fingerprints. The bar was heavy and warm in my hands.

Most people had never seen a gold bar up close. I wasn't one of them. A drug kingpin, Carlos the Armadillo, whose cabal I'd infiltrated, kept hundreds of the things around his lair. He had a problem with banks, thinking the CIA was after his money.

In the end, once he was arrested, his fears became reality when the CIA confiscated the gold. He was not happy.

The girls and Edna Lou surrounded me, which was difficult in the tiny building. Kelly had her cell out and was calling Rex. It disappointed me a little because it seemed like an excellent clue. But a large gold bar is not easy to hide on your person—especially in July.

"Wow!" the four Kaitlyns exclaimed

Ava reached out to touch it, but I pulled it back. "Fingerprints," I said.

The girl nodded and withdrew her hand.

"Let's go outside," Kelly suggested. "It's too hot in here. Who wants to play a game?"

The girls screamed and ran outside. They were playing red rover before we even suggested it.

In the sunlight, the gold was dazzling. Kelly, Edna Lou, and I formed a circle around it, staring. I had to admit, it was beautiful. Hypnotic even. I lifted it to look at the inscription on the top.

A little llama was embossed in the middle, next to the letters M. P.

"It's the fortune!" Kelly's voice squeaked. "It does exist!"

"Why was it here?" I wondered out loud.

Edna was frozen in place, never taking her eyes off the bar.

"Edna Lou?" I nudged.

The spell broke, and she looked from Kelly to me. "I don't know. It wasn't there before. I clean the whole building every Tuesday. I even moved the filing cabinets to get underneath. If this had been there, I would have seen it."

"Which means that Ike must have brought it here." My mind was racing.

"Can I hold it?" Edna Lou asked.

I handed it to her, using the cloth. "Don't touch it directly." I understood the lure of the gold.

"Why would Ike bring it here?" I asked. "Did he tell you he was coming over?"

Edna Lou's fingers tightened around the treasure as her eyes welled up. "What? Oh. Um, yes. He said he had something to talk about."

"He must've found the treasure," Kelly said. "He was bringing it here to show you."

Tears streamed down her cheeks, but she said nothing.

"Did he say anything else?" I pressed. "Something that could give us a hint?"

The woman shook her head. If Ike did say anything more, she wasn't sharing it.

A police cruiser pulled up, and Rex stepped out of the passenger side. Officer Kevin Dooley continued to sit behind the wheel while eating marshmallows from a plastic baggie.

Rex held out his hand to Edna Lou, but she hesitated. It was pretty obvious that she didn't want to give up the gold bar. After a few seconds, she reluctantly handed it over.

I described where we'd found it and admitted that my prints might be on it from when I picked it up.

"Show me exactly where you found it," Rex said.

Inside the cabin, I took him to where I'd found Ike's body. Rex pulled on some latex gloves and got down on his hands and knees. He shone a flashlight under the cabinet, and got to his feet, shoving the furniture aside.

There was nothing there. That was too bad. It would've been nice to find a note that implicated the killer and explained where the rest of the bars were.

"Did you search Ike's house?" I said.

Rex could've rolled his eyes, because duh, of course he searched the victim's house. But he didn't, because he's awesome.

"We did. But we must have missed something. I'll take Officer Dooley and head back over there."

I groaned. "He won't be very helpful."

Rex thought about this for a second. "You might be right. I'll take someone else."

I grinned. He was talking about me.

"I'll ask Dr. Body to help."

My smile vanished.


It was very difficult to get the girls to leave when their parents came. We'd asked them to keep the discovery to themselves, and I had no doubt they would. My troop had no problem practicing discretion.

We helped Edna Lou clean up. Tears rimmed her eyes more than once, reminding me of the loss of her cousin. It also must have been a shock to have the legendary treasure this close, only to find the one person with information about it was dead. Okay, that sounded harsh. This woman lost a family member. I'd have to remember that.

"Thanks again," I said as we finished. "I know the girls loved it."

"I loved it," Kelly said.

Somehow, I knew it wasn't the cleaning up part she was talking about.

"Thank you for cleaning the scene of the…of the…" She didn't finish. Tears started to run down her cheeks for the second time. I'd guessed that the shock finally wore off and she was mourning the loss of her cousin.

"It's okay," I said quickly. "We were happy to help out."

The woman wiped her tears away looked up at me. "I'd really like to see that map. I could use a distraction."

Kelly patted her shoulder. "We'll get it to you."

As we walked back to our cars, I couldn't help getting excited. Stuff was happening! Cool stuff. Well, except for Ike's murder, that was.

"Want to come over for a glass of wine?" I asked.

She nodded. "I'll pick up Finn and meet you there."

Twenty minutes later, Finn was sitting on the kitchen floor, playing with a big plastic spoon and various pots and pans. Philby, who'd taken a liking to the baby, sat next to her as if supervising. Martini climbed into one of the pots and fell asleep. The fact that a small child was smacking that pot with a spoon didn't seem to bother her.

I had made a copy of the map, one page for each side. I laid these out, side by side on the breakfast bar, and we studied them.

"Mehitable, or Mimi," Kelly said, "lived here. In the house where your sisters-in-law now live and work." She ran her finger toward where my house would be and stopped. "And here's where the map was."

"Which was, at the time, her brother's farm."

I looked in the phone book and found Ike Murphy's address. I didn't have a landline, but old people still did. Turned out, Ike lived across town, next door to the zoo.

"We should go over there," I said.

"Didn't you tell me Rex and Soo Jin are there, searching for more gold?"

I gave her a look. "When did I tell you that?"

"When we were walking to our cars."

"Maybe they aren't there anymore."

Kelly's right eyebrow rose, "Is that a risk you're willing to take?"

Good point. Even though Rex wanted to solve the mystery of Mad Mimi's fortune, he was there right now investigating a murder. He probably wouldn't consider the two things linked…even though I thought they were. Did I want to annoy him right now? I was really good at that.

I smiled at Finn, who had put one of the pot lids on Philby's head and was hitting it with the spoon. The cat wasn't mad at *her* but looked at *me* with murder in her eyes.

"When was the last time Finn went to the zoo?"

# CHAPTER TEN

———

"Why is he doing that?" Kelly held Finn away from the glass where Mr. Fancy Pants, a king vulture, was throwing himself at the glass in my direction.

She should know the answer. My troop and I had a history with the raptor. Originally from the National Zoo in DC, the bird had helped me with a troublesome Yakuza member during a trip to our nation's capital.

He had a crack-like addiction to Girl Scout Cookies.

"I may have been visiting him." I shrugged. "In the off hours. It's possible I may have brought cookies."

Finn squealed with delight, clapping her hands at the antics of the large, googly-eyed bird. Kelly tightened her grip.

If you'd never seen a king vulture before, it was a startling sight. A large white bird with black on the wings, the raptor had what appeared to be a hairless purplish head with bits of stubble where I guessed feathers would normally be. A bright beak with a brilliantly orange wattle hanging over it and large googly eyes gave it a deranged, muppety sort of appearance.

Children were starting to surround us as their mothers tugged them back in fear.

"I have animal crackers in my diaper bag," Kelly hissed at me.

"Then you should probably walk away quickly because they are known for their sense of smell."

Kelly rushed away with the stroller to the next exhibit. Fancy Pants quieted down, and the children, disappointed, wandered away.

I knelt down in front of the glass. The bird came over and eyed me suspiciously. Or maybe it was affectionately. It was hard to tell when the eyes went in different directions like that.

"I'll bring you some cookies later," I whispered to the glass. "But only if you behave."

The bird stared at me before hopping back to the big branch I usually sat on with him when I broke in at night. He climbed up and sat there, staring out.

A month or so ago, the bird was loaned out to our zoo. The girls were delighted because they adored him, and I paid a significant fee to "adopt" him. As a result, the zoo let me visit. Most of the time I broke in after hours and picked the lock to his cage. I'd smuggle him cookies, and we'd have a nice chat.

He was an excellent listener.

I caught up with Kelly and Finn as they were heading to the reptile house. The zoo was only open until 6, and the time was drawing near. By now, Rex had to be done searching Ike's house.

"Mama!" Finn shouted as we neared the gift shop exit.

"She's talking?" I marveled.

Kelly nodded. "She is. *Mama* is her first word."

"Merrr-yyy" I said slowly and loudly to my goddaughter. "What are you doing?"

"I want her next word to be Merry." I shrugged. "Merrr-yyy."

But Finn wasn't having it. She just shouted "MAMA" and pointed to a statue a few feet away.

"I think she's saying llama," I teased Kelly.

A large, lifelike sculpture of a llama with a surprised look on its face stood a few feet away.

"She doesn't know what a llama is." Kelly bit her lip.

This was a lie. A few months ago I'd bought Finn a board book about a llama with intestinal gas issues. I happened to know that Robert read it to her every night.

"That must be new," Kelly said as she walked her daughter over to the statue. "We were here last month, and I don't think it was here then."

"MAMA!" Finn shouted again as she clapped her hands at the statue.

I stepped closer to examine it. The llama was looking straight ahead, eyes open wide, tongue hanging out of the right side of its mouth. He looked demented.

"Look!" Kelly pointed at the plaque on the ground in front of it.

*Tinkles the Llama, beloved pet of Mehitable Peters.*

"When? Why?" I had trouble putting words together.

This was too much of a coincidence. Why did this appear here, now? I stared at the writing to make sure I was reading it correctly. There was some very small print, and I had to crouch down to read it.

*Donated by Ferguson Taxidermy—Where Your Pet Lives On Forever!*

I read this out loud, in case I was hallucinating.

"Randi and Ronni donated this?" Kelly asked. "What a strange coincidence."

I shook my head. "I don't think its coincidence at all."

An announcement came over the loudspeaker telling us the zoo was closing and to please visit the gift shop on our way out.

"It's six," I said. "Their shop will be closing too."

"Let's go tomorrow," Kelly suggested. "I'm free first thing in the morning."

We agreed. I took a picture of the statue and on the way out bought a stuffed king vulture for Finn. She chewed happily on his wattle while we drove out the exit and around back to the address listed for Ike.

A tiny white house sat on a large lot surrounded by trees. It didn't have one single neighbor. Maybe that was why Ike liked it. Privacy was more important to some people than having a big house.

We drove by slowly to make sure Rex wasn't there. It was deserted. With no neighbors, it would be fairly easy to check out. Kelly parked a block away and got out the stroller. She would walk Finn around the neighborhood, and if she saw anything suspicious or Rex (I wasn't sure which would be worse), she'd call me.

The front door was level with the sidewalk. There were windows on each side of the door. I walked around back via the driveway on the left. There was another door to the driveway and sliding glass doors facing the backyard. No garage, no shed. Just the house.

Peering in through the sliding glass doors didn't tell me much. A simple kitchen with a small table and two chairs were all I could see. My guess from the layout was that there'd be one bedroom, a small living room, and a bathroom on the other side.

A bunch of pamphlets on the table promoted the Who's There Historical Society. There wasn't a gold bar in sight.

What did I expect? That there'd be a pile of gold with a note that said who killed Mehitable and *here's a puppy, just for your trouble*?

A lion roared, and I jumped backward into a defensive stance. Oh. Right. The zoo was in this guy's backyard. And what kind of defensive position would stop a lion attack anyway? I was getting rusty.

Pulling on a pair of bright yellow cleaning gloves (what? They were handy), I gently took hold of the sliding glass door and pulled.

It was open.

Two things were happening here. Either Officer Kevin Dooley had been with Rex and Soo Jin and left the door open, or someone else had the same idea as me. There was no lock on the outside, and it didn't look like it had been tampered with. Which meant someone got in through another door and exited this way.

Had Rex surprised someone? Why didn't he check to make sure the door was locked? It didn't sound like Rex. Or Soo Jin. The coroner had to have some police training. Right?

Well, their mistake was my gain. Was it breaking and entering if the door was unlocked? I entered and closed the door silently behind me. And waited.

Here was where spies got caught. Upon breaking into an unknown location, you had to wait to make sure no one heard you. If there was someone home, you beat a quick retreat. If not, you could proceed…but with extreme caution, because people with something to hide rarely left doors unlocked.

To my surprise, the house was neat as a pin. The kitchen was spotless and smelled of cleansers. Not one dish languished in the sink. There weren't even any water stains in the stainless-steel sink.

I started with the cupboards first, opening each drawer and door as quietly as I could. Nothing looked out of sorts. In fact, if I didn't know any better, I'd say this house was totally staged. Everything was tidily stacked with not so much as a dust speck anywhere. Either Ike was very neat, or he didn't live here at all. I took that idea and shoved it into the back of my mind.

After crawling under the table and chairs to see if anything was taped to the seat or table, I got up and looked around. Was this a slab house with no basement? I'd heard of prefab houses after World War II being set up on slabs of cement. But I'd never really been in one.

There wasn't any other way out of the kitchen but through to the living room. It was small, cut in half by a doorway to a bedroom and a bathroom. A clean but worn leather recliner sat in front of a huge, state-of-the-art smart TV. A small end table completed the furniture suite. The floor had brand-new carpet. I'd have to remember to rub out my footprints on my way out.

The room was dark because the shades were drawn. I waited a moment for my eyes to adjust. Turning on a light might alert someone to my presence. Checking my phone for any messages from Kelly was a bust. Which was good news.

The TV was mounted on a wall. I had to use the flashlight on my cell to check the back of it, but I didn't see anything unusual. I walked around the carpet, checking to see if any corners pulled up where messages might be hidden. Nope. It was tacked on tight.

The table had nothing on it but a remote for the TV. I checked the underside. Nothing. Very slowly I opened the recliner and got down on the floor. I couldn't see anything underneath, and it was hard to feel around with a thick rubber glove on. After coming up empty, I moved on to the bedroom.

Once again, the room was spotless and Spartan. One twin-sized bed divided the little room in half. There was one dresser and one nightstand and one closet. I'd have to take a little more time in here.

If I was asked which room I'd most likely find secret stuff, I'd say the bedroom every time. People put their most precious possessions in the room they slept in, for extra security. I'd found everything from nuclear codes to stacks of passports in bedrooms. Once, I even found a boa constrictor named Heather.

This was why I always kept my stuff in my unfinished basement. My theory was that if a burglar was looking for something important, they'd skip the basement entirely, thinking if I didn't put any effort into finishing the room, I certainly wouldn't keep valuables there.

After checking the carpets, I made quick work of the nightstand and bed. The closet was easier than I thought it would be because Ike only owned two pair of shoes, two pair of pants, and two shirts. Huh. There wasn't even a jacket or winter coat. That was strange for Iowa. It was possible he stored his things somewhere else, but the closet was almost completely empty. There was no reason not to keep coats in there.

I rapped on each wall and studied the one shelf, but found nothing. The dresser was next. There had to be something in there.

There were three drawers. The first one held two pair of boxer shorts and two pair of white tube socks. A pattern was developing around the number two. No, wait. He'd been wearing clothes when murdered, so there must've been three of everything. Still, how often did this guy do laundry? I hadn't seen a washer and dryer yet.

The second drawer held one belt. One. That was all. Which meant Ike had two. I ran my fingers over it to see if it had hidden pockets. Nope. I pulled out the drawer above it and turned it over. Nothing was taped to the bottom. I pulled out the second and examined it. Nothing.

Something was very wrong here. Surely Rex and Soo Jin had seen it too. This house rang hollow. It was as if no one lived here. I'd found food in the kitchen, but it was all in cans. Now this.

I turned my attention to the bottom drawer and immediately wished I hadn't. It was full of women's wigs in all shapes and sizes—long, curly, short, wavy, and every color imaginable. I tried to picture Ike's head without the axe in it. I got the impression he was bald.

I pulled out the wigs and set them on the floor around me. I didn't like the second layer any better.

Thong panties and push-up bras, again, of every size and color. They seemed brand new. Did Ike like to dress up as a woman? If so, why all the different sizes? I found thongs in size zero and XXL. The bras ranged from size 30A to 50DDD.

I replaced everything as I remembered it. This was all wrong. My spy-dy senses were tingling. Maybe because this didn't make any sense. After checking under the drawer and behind the dresser, I made my way to the bathroom.

Standing in the doorway, I gasped audibly, clapping my hand over my mouth. The bathroom was neat as a pin. But there was a flamingo skeleton in the tub, looking back at me.

Like the other rooms, the toilet was pristine and the shower looked brand new. A pair of fluffy white hand towels that looked like they'd never been used hung on a rod. The sink was polished until it shone. The floor had tile, so no secrets there. There was no cupboard under the sink because it sat on a pedestal.

I checked the medicine cabinet and found one bottle of aspirin. From the intact plastic around the lid, I'd say it had never been opened. There wasn't any toothbrush or razor. It was such a small room that I had to close the door to turn around.

Skeletons kind of creeped me out. That didn't bode well for a woman whose fiancé's sisters were taxidermists. But I'd never seen any in their home. Had Ike gotten the flamingo from them? Or had it come from the zoo?

Maybe it was fake? Very carefully, I touched the beak…or bill…whatever it was. It seemed real. What was holding it together? I drew back. The thing seemed to be looking right at me, even though it didn't have any eyes.

Instead, I checked the plain white shower curtain. Nothing. There was one brand-new bar of soap in a dish on the side of the tub, but no shampoo or anything else. Not that he needed shampoo if he was bald. Still, the whole house was devoid of…things.

Except for a bunch of wigs, some women's underwear, and the flamingo skeleton, this place looked like no one lived here. I reached out to touch the flamingo again for reasons I couldn't fully explain.

It toppled to the tub floor in a deafening clatter. Bones came apart as they fell and broke apart upon landing. It sounded like a bunch of wood blocks hitting the floor. I froze. I was pretty confident that no one was in here with me, but you never knew.

For a moment I toyed with trying to put the flamingo back together. How was I going to do that? Instead, I just apologized to the skull, which lay upside down in the tub.

And that was when I saw it. A tiny piece of folded paper taped to the skull.

My cell buzzed with a text from Kelly. She told me to hurry up—she'd run out of neighborhood, and the lions were freaking Finn out.

I grabbed the flamingo skull and ran for it, scuffing my footprints on the carpet in the living room as I went. I dove out the back of the sliding glass doors, and after making sure the coast was clear, walked casually around to the front sidewalk.

Kelly was waiting for me. She was staring at my T-shirt. "What's that?" She pointed to the flamingo skull–shaped bump near my belly.

"Let's go," I said as I lifted Finn out of the stroller to hide the bump.

Once we were in the car and driving off, I told Kelly everything about the house.

"Maybe Edna Lou cleaned it out?"

I shook my head as I pulled the skull from underneath my shirt. "In two days? I don't think it's doable."

"Maybe he didn't live here?" Kelly asked.

"That's an interesting theory." Did we get it wrong? Search the wrong house? Did Ike live somewhere else and keep this place to store his girly underthings and bird bones?

I turned the skull over and examined it. I wanted to avoid anyone seeing it through the car window.

We arrived at my house in minutes. I turned the dead bolt on the front door, just in case Rex decided to pop over unannounced. The last thing I needed was for him to find me with a flamingo skull. I wasn't sure how I could explain the coincidence of having it on me.

We gave Finn some Cheerios and more pots and pans to bang on before setting the skull on the breakfast bar. That was when I realized I was still wearing the yellow gloves. I took them off. I'd wipe the skull clean before returning it…if I even did that.

What was Rex going to think when he found the pile of bones in the tub? Hopefully, he'd notice the unlocked door and think kids had broken in. As long as he didn't know it was me. I wasn't technically authorized to investigate this murder.

I peeled the tape off the piece of paper and unfolded it.

"It's the map!" Kelly said.

It was the map. The same treasure map we had, with one very significant difference. This map had a huge *X* on it. And that *X* was in Rex's front yard.

# CHAPTER ELEVEN

———

The next morning I was deep in thought, studying the map. I sat in my living room, looking across the street to Rex's house, wondering just how I was going to search the yard.

It wasn't like I could pass it off as anything innocent. What excuse could I have? Although, Rex did want to help me find the treasure. But telling him would require an answer to how did I find this new map?

There wasn't a single hole in his yard. If that was where Ike got the gold bar, how did he manage it without leaving a hole (or several)? Did the gold bar come from somewhere else? If so, why was there an *X* marking Rex's yard?

I held the map up to the light to determine if the *X* was old or new. An indent on the other side told me it was written in pencil.

Philby jumped up into the large picture window. Her pupils were the size of dinner plates, and she was fixated on something at Rex's house. This wasn't unusual. Last year my fiancé had a mouse problem. And even after the exterminator came and went, my obese house cat was always trying to escape to get over there.

One time she slipped into the sleeve of my coat and ran outside. It looked like my coat was trying to run away from home. Another time she got into the garbage bag that had to go out to the dumpster. Fortunately, I bought cheap bags that ripped under her weight, leaving an angry cat sitting in a pile of garbage in my kitchen.

She never just made a break for it when we opened the front door. I guess that was far too pedestrian for the wily likes of her.

*Yeooooooooow!*

Philby was now throwing herself at the window, which was hard to do with all her bulk. She basically had to lean back and jump toward it. It was like watching a medicine ball hit a window in slow motion.

And it gave me an idea…

*   *   *

"Merry?" Rex closed the car door from his driveway and walked over to me. "What's going on?"

"Philby got out and ran over here!" I tried to sound desperate.

He stared at me. "And why do you have a metal detector?"

He had me there. It probably wasn't my brightest idea, since it didn't have anything to do with my now missing cat. Well, she wasn't missing. Just circling the house trying to find a way in.

"I saw this thing on PBS about how people find all kinds of things in their front yards and thought I'd start with yours." I switched off the device and pasted on my most innocent smile.

It was a terrible story. And one I didn't think I'd even need. Rex usually worked until five or six, and it was only noon. I'd hoped I'd be able to scan the front yard quickly and put the equipment away before Rex ever got home. I was going to mark any spot I found with a dandelion.

Philby trotted around the side of the house for the eleventh time since we'd gotten there, yowling all the way. Rex retrieved her and scratched under her chin, making her eyes go wide like a mental wildebeest.

"Oh." I took my cat from him. "There she is. Bad kitty."

Philby narrowed her eyes at me. She didn't like being a pawn in my intrigues unless they included tuna.

Rex sighed. "You think the treasure is in my yard. Why?"

"Because the map was in mine." That was true. "It's common knowledge that often, the treasure isn't far from the map." That part I made up.

A grin tugged at the corner of his lips. "And did you find any treasure?"

I shook my head. "No. Not so much as a nail. Your yard is clean. You're welcome."

He nodded as if he knew this all along. "Why don't I run and get some takeout and bring it over?"

I jumped at the idea. "Yes! I'll get everything ready." I hightailed it out of there before he'd come up with another question.

Philby did not like being dumped, unceremoniously, in the kitchen. But since she'd been a good little henchman, I opened up a can of tuna for her. Martini came running, so I split it between two dishes.

By the time Rex showed up, I'd set a table in the backyard with plates, napkins, and two glasses of iced tea. The heat wasn't too bad for July. It felt like a picnic. I liked summer in Iowa. To be honest, I liked all the seasons in my home state. And while we could get super-humid summers and bitterly cold, snowy winters, it was still my favorite place to be. And I'd been to both the French and Italian Rivieras. Twice.

"How was work?" I mumbled through a mouthful of chicken.

Ever the gentleman, Rex swallowed before answering. "We had a break-in at a property by the zoo."

"Oh?" I asked as I poured honey onto a biscuit.

Rex nodded, studying me. "Yes. It's one of Ike Murphy's places."

*One of?*

"He had more than one place?"

"He did. The man had a house about a block from here. And a tiny house by Obladi Zoo that he owned. We think he lived in the first place and used the second for who knows what."

"Why do you think that?"

"Because the house near here was lived in, and the other seemed to be staged."

I suggested,. "Could it have been the killer, searching for something?"

My fiancé considered this for a moment, and I took the opportunity to fill my mouth with mashed potatoes and gravy.

"The staged house was broken into," he said at last.

"Was it trashed?" I tried to throw him off.

"No, it wasn't trashed. In fact, the only reason we think it was hit was the unlocked back door and the pile of flamingo bones in the tub."

There were several ways I could react. But a normal person would only react one way.

"Flamingo bones? Did you say flamingo bones?" My mind went to the flamingo skull I'd hidden under my bed.

If Rex thought I was the guilty party, he didn't say it. "That's right. No one is sure how they got there. The zoo isn't missing a flamingo."

I shrugged. "Maybe he collects them? You could probably order it online. You can get anything online."

This was true. A Chechen strongman I'd been surveilling once ordered the car from *Chitty Chitty Bang Bang*. On eBay.

Rex gave up. "It's technically not illegal to own flamingo bones. But they were all attached to each other in the form of a proper skeleton when I first went by there."

"Do you have any leads?"

"Merry, I…"

I held my hands up. "I'm not interfering, but I do think this murder and Mad Mimi's murder are related. And you and I were going to investigate that, remember?"

"I remember." He pulled out his cell and looked at it.

"You said the two of us would work together on this. And we haven't had one moment to do so."

"Well, our luck just changed." He put his phone back into his pocket. "Let's put the food away. Sheriff Carnack has some news for us."

\* \* \*

"Here you go." Carnack shoved a file folder toward us, and I opened it.

I shoved the brittle newspaper clipping aside. We'd already read it at the library. The yellowed pages of what was the equivalent of a police report, back in the day, was written in perfect penmanship.

"The man who wrote this report claimed it was murder." I looked up at Carnack. "But I thought it was deemed an accident?"

The sheriff pointed at the file. "That's because that report wasn't written by the marshal. It was written by a Pinkerton detective."

I looked questioningly at Rex.

"At that time," he said, "the only law was a town marshal. There might have been a watchman too, but neither of them would be trained in murder investigations."

Carnack agreed. "In most cases, the governor would offer a reward, which brought every detective from the Midwest in to investigate in hopes of making money. Pinkertons were private detectives with the Pinkerton agency, and one of them came here."

"So"—I frowned at the report—"there were several people investigating one murder?"

Rex spoke up. "Yes. Kind of like when you investigate something I'm investigating. It muddies the waters. Makes it tough to find answers."

He had me there.

"The town marshal thought it was an accident, but the Pinkertons thought it was murder? Didn't they talk to each other?"

The sheriff sighed. "In most cases, since he wasn't trained to deal with murder, justice was meted out as quickly as possible to put the mess behind them. In some cases, when they had a suspect, a group of vigilantes would grab the suspect and hang him before a trial could take place. The marshal probably didn't want to deal with that, so he declared it an accident."

"That doesn't make any sense," I grumbled.

"Did the detective have any theories?" Rex pulled the folder over to him.

Sheriff Carnack nodded. "Billy the Axeman."

"Billy the Axeman?" I had to ask.

Rex leaned back in his chair. "There were a number of axe murders in the Midwest during this time. People didn't really know about serial killers. But a few tied the Villisca Axe Murders, along with some others in Colorado Springs, Blue

Island, Illinois, to name a few, to Billy the Axeman. The theory is that he was a transient who traveled by train and found his victims in the night."

I stared at both of them. Everyone in Iowa knew about the Villisca Axe Murders. It had been a crime in the early 1900s, and the killer was never caught.

"Billy the Axeman? That's a terrible name for a serial killer! It isn't scary! It sounds like a cartoon character who helps people when they get stuck inside wooden boxes!" I shook my head.

Rex rolled his eyes. "*That's* what you got out of this?"

"If it's Billy the Axeman, and no one has ever found out who he was, how can we solve it? At least we can make fun of his name." The girls would probably agree with me. I wasn't sure I should tell them. After all, who needed Betty the Axeman?

Carnack leaned forward. "I don't think it was Billy the Axeman. I think it was someone local. The modus operandi is different. Billy did certain things like cover mirrors and windows, cover the victims' faces, killed them in their sleep. This was, in my opinion, meant to look like it was part of those crimes."

Rex and I looked at the file again. The Pinkerton agent, a man named Smith, filled in the details. Mehitable was found in the dining room. She was dressed in day clothes and had shoes on. She even had a purse in her right hand. The woman had been getting ready to go out.

"Some detective," I scoffed. "If he thought it really was Billy, he sure didn't pay attention to the state of the victim."

Rex shrugged. "He was just here to earn the reward."

"Did he get it?" I asked.

"There's no evidence that he did," Carnack said. "I wonder why he pinned it on Billy?"

"So, who did it?" I threw up my hands.

Rex studied the file. "Smith interviewed her brother, Eustace, and a cousin, Peggy McMurtry. Both were in town during the murders but had no alibi."

"Eustace," the sheriff said, "was a pillar of the community. He was a successful farmer and deacon in the church, and he helped the town with incorporation. His wife was the church organist, and she raised five children. I doubt that the marshal looked any further."

I frowned at the file in Rex's hands. "Peggy? There was no mention of a Peggy in the diary."

Rex shook his head. "Doesn't say much other than they decided she wasn't a suspect."

It always came down to family, didn't it? They were usually the first investigated. I wondered if Edna Lou knew anything about Peggy. The story we learned in school never mentioned anyone else in the Peters family.

"Mehitable was killed in the Peters' house. That's where your sisters live and work now," I said to Rex. "Maybe we should pay them a visit. I'd like to see the dining room."

We thanked Sheriff Carnack and headed for the parking lot. Rex seemed tense. But then, he always acted like that when we were going to see his family. That seemed unfair. Randi and Ronni were his sisters. And they were going to be my sisters.

"Maybe I should drop you off at home and you can go see the twins," Rex said. "I should check in at the office…"

"Oh no you're not," I insisted. "Besides, I need you if we are going to reenact the murder scene.

Five minutes later we were walking through the door. You might think that I always say it took five minutes to get somewhere in Who's There. But it literally takes only five minutes. Unless there's gridlock because a farmer drives a combine into town. And that really only happens once or twice a year.

"Rexley!" Randi came out of the back room and hurled herself into her brother's arms.

It was hard to get used to the fact that his real name was Rexley. I'd tried to use it myself once or twice, but he made it clear that it was Rex, and only Rex. I smiled as I saw his petite and plump sister hug him. Then she came at me.

"And Merry! I'm so happy to see you both!" She crushed me in an embrace.

"For crying out loud!" Ronni joined us. "You're interrupting our work!"

This twin made no effort to hug her brother or me. Instead she folded her arms over her chest, kind of like an inverted un-hug. The only way I could tell these two apart was that one was happy and smiled and the other was surly and scowling.

Randi ignored her sister. "This is the perfect time for you to stop by! I had another thought for the wedding!"

Ronni rolled her eyes but made no move to leave. Randi motioned for us to follow her into the next room. I was taking note. The entryway was a room, and I wondered if it was original to the place.

"Was this the dining room?" I asked as we made our way into a room that, for some reason, was filled with warthogs in various states of dress.

Randi turned to a wardrobe and pulled something out. She spun on her heel and with eyes shining, presented it to us.

"Ferrets?" I asked.

Two of the weasels were dressed as the bride and groom, standing back to back as if they were about to pace off for a duel.

"Is that supposed to be me?" Rex pointed at the groom.

"I was thinking we could put this on the altar." Randi added. "It's the unity candle!"

"What's a unity candle?" I asked.

"It's a candle you both light together," Randi explained.

"What are you"—Ronni snorted—"an idiot?"

Rex glared at his sister, who threw her hands up in the air and stalked out of the room, shouting, "It's a fair question!"

Randi patted my arm apologetically as she pointed to the animals' heads. "They're each one candle." She pulled them apart then pushed them back together. "You light one each, individually, and then push them together! Voilà!"

There was a long, uncomfortable silence. Randi's face fell. She'd tried several times to contribute to the ceremony, but everything she'd made had been dismissed. I couldn't do it to her again.

"You nailed it! Great idea! We'll do that!" I said.

If Rex was surprised, he didn't show it.

"You like it?" Randi's eyes shone with joy.

I nodded. "I love it! We love it, right?" I nudged Rex with my foot.

"It's perfect," he agreed.

Which was good because otherwise I'd have to overrule him.

Personally, I wasn't fond of the ferret candle. But I was fond of Randi. And that had to count for something.

"I'm so glad you love it!" Randi jumped up and down gleefully before crushing both of us together in one huge hug.

"It's about time you liked something!" Ronni shouted from another room.

"I have a great idea about the pew bows!" Randi said quickly. "Since your colors are green and white, I was thinking of those green tree snakes! We could tie them into bows! And albino snakes for the color white!"

I stared at her. "You're on a roll!"

You might be thinking I was crazy, but I was fairly certain she wouldn't be able to find these snakes. Although I did wonder what the Methodists would think of snake pew bows. I'd figure out how to deal with that later.

Randi ran out of the room, presumably to order dead snakes. Rex walked the perimeter of the room, studying it.

"Do you think this was the dining room?" I asked.

He nodded. "I'd say it was." He pointed to the room his sister had just gone into. "That's the kitchen, and the measurements look right."

I'd never really looked at this house before. I'd only seen the bizarre animals that filled its rooms. Now I had to visualize it like it was at the turn of the century. It was like being in a new house.

My fiancé walked around the room before stopping and pointing at the corner to the right of the kitchen door.

"That's where she was found." He looked around and found a stuffed German shepherd standing like a person, wearing a yellow raincoat with a purple umbrella over its arm.

I watched with surprise as he laid the animal down on its back, head in the corner, feet near the table.

"This is the position of Mimi's body, according to the report."

I found an axe, believe it or not, in the hands of a bear dressed as a lumberjack, and handed it to him. Rex placed the cutting edge next to the dog's head with the handle parallel to the wall.

It looked like the dog had walked in on something he shouldn't have and was murdered for it.

"Was she coming out of, or going into, the kitchen?"

Rex walked around the table, frowned, then walked the other way. "I'm not sure. She had her purse, and the theory was she was going out. She could've come into this room to go to the kitchen, or come out of the kitchen in order to leave the house."

We stared at the dog body, on its back, head in the corner. The killer could've come from either direction. There was no way of knowing what really happened unless we had a time machine, in which case, we wouldn't have to solve the murder—cuz duh, time machine!

"What are you doing?" Ronni shouted from behind us, causing both of us to jump and spin. I, of course, landed in a perfect defensive position. Rex hadn't been startled at all.

"When you bought the house," Rex said, "did the real estate agent tell you about the murder that occurred here?"

Ronni snapped. "Of course she did! It was a long time ago. Who cares?"

Randi joined us. "She said that someone named Mad Mimi was killed here about one hundred years ago. Why?"

"We are trying to solve the case," I said. "So we decided to reenact it to figure out what really happened. The only problem is, we don't know for sure what position she was in."

"Well, that's easy," Randi said.

She moved the dog aside and lay down where it had been. Only this time, she lay on her side, facing the kitchen.

"Why do you think that's what happened?" Rex asked.

Ronni stormed out of the room and to our complete surprise, returned with a photo. She shoved it into Rex's hands before leaving again.

"Oh, wow," Rex muttered as Randi and I closed in to look over his shoulder. "It's a picture of the murder scene."

There, in grainy black and white, was Mehitable, in the exact position on the floor as my future sister-in-law.

# CHAPTER TWELVE

———

"How did you get this?" I gasped.

Randi shrugged. "In a drawer when we moved in."

"I didn't realize any photos were taken," Rex said. "That wasn't usual back in the day."

I took the picture from him. Sure enough, Mehitable was lying on her right side, facing the kitchen. She was fully dressed, and the cord of a small purse was wound around her left wrist.

"Can we keep this for a little bit?" Rex asked his sister.

"Of course. I'll need it back eventually. To beef up business we were going to stage the whole thing here in the corner, using a swan for Mad Mimi. Ronni thought it would bring in tourists."

To be honest, neither one of us was surprised by this statement. Although I must admit, my stomach clenched a little at the idea, knowing that Edna Lou also wanted this house to be a museum to Mimi's murder.

"I think"—Rex pulled out his cell "that we need an expert opinion."

\* \* \*

Dr. Body arrived within minutes. We briefed Soo Jin on the story, and she studied the picture. In a strange and twisted way…this was interesting.

We returned the dog to its side to match the photo. Soo Jin walked between the corner and the kitchen door, and then from the main entrance to the corner. Finally, she knelt down by the dog and looked around.

"Okay." Soo Jin stood up and dusted off her hands.

That was when she really looked around her for the first time. The look on her face as she saw two otters in tuxedos knitting, a moose in a varsity jacket getting ready to kick a soccer ball, and two vultures committing arson to a dollar store, was priceless. She started to walk around, examining each and every piece of whimsy that crowded this room.

"This is *amazing*!" She said at last. "You are real artists!"

Randi beamed, basking in the glow that was Soo Jin. "Thank you! It's so nice to be appreciated!"

The doctor asked, "Do you have anything with turkeys? I really like turkeys."

"I have just the thing! Tell me, do you like history? Because I've got these turkeys dressed as former presidents playing jump rope that…"

Rex cleared his throat. That was all he needed to do. I, on the other hand, wanted her to keep going.

Randi winked at the coroner. "I'll show you in a bit, dear."

Soo Jin snapped back to the present. "Oh! Right! Sorry."

She walked me over to the corner and had me face the kitchen. Then she ran around behind me, raising an imaginary axe over her head and bringing it down on mine. I dutifully crumpled to the floor.

"That's how I think this went down," Soo Jin said. "Death was most likely instantaneous. There aren't any distinguishing footprints, so I'm guessing the killer walked the other way around the table…" Which she then demonstrated. "Before walking out the door."

"She didn't try to defend herself?" Rex asked.

Soo Jin studied the photo one more time. "I don't think so, but it's hard to be one hundred percent sure. I also think the killer was taller than her."

That was when I remembered that Randi had said "them"—pictures, plural. I grabbed the photo and found two more stuck together to the back. The second picture was from the waist up.

"See?" Soo Jin pointed to the dead woman's arms and hands. "No defensive wounds. I think she was shocked and it happened very quickly."

"Could it have been thrown?" I asked. "So she wouldn't see that coming until too late?"

Rex picked up the axe and stood in the kitchen doorway, pretending to hurl it overhead. The ceilings were too low. It didn't happen that way.

"Is this the original ceiling?" I asked. "Maybe they were higher and over the years people lowered it?"

Randi shook her head. "We were told that the ceiling was old when we bought the place."

I walked over to the spot where Rex stood and looked up. There was a strange mark on the ceiling, which, considering all the water damages spots, was tough to notice. I grabbed a stepladder and moved closer.

"There are a couple of holes in the ceiling." I took a picture with my cell. "Maybe from nails?"

Soo Jin nodded. "Probably hooks. They used to hang herbs from the ceiling to dry them out."

I climbed back down and set the ladder aside. "I guess nothing out of the ordinary then."

"What did you think you'd find?" Rex seemed amused.

"A gash or dent from the axe." I swung the axe up over my head, and it smacked into the ceiling.

"Sorry." I handed the weapon back to my fiancé.

"Can we borrow these photos?" Rex asked Randi.

"Of course! Now"—she turned to Soo Jin—"would you like to see the turkey presidents?"

Rex and I fled back to the reasonable sanity of his car.

"It was definitely murder then," I said, as if trying to convince myself.

"I'd say so," Rex replied. "I just don't see how she could fall on top of an axe and end up on her side with the axe in her forehead. It had to be murder."

"And the only suspects we have are Eustace and Peggy McMurtry—the cousin," I mused.

"Looks like it," Rex said. "Eustace had motive and opportunity. He had a farm, so he probably knew how to handle an axe."

Something seemed wrong about this theory. "Eustace displayed no hostility towards his sister. He had money and didn't need hers."

Rex adjusted in his seat to face me. "Murders, in my experience, are over love or money in most cases. And just because someone has money, doesn't mean they don't need more. People are naturally greedy. Eustace may have been well-off, but that doesn't mean he didn't want more."

"I suppose…" I wasn't quite convinced. "She hasn't found a will, but Edna told me that it was rumored Mad Mimi left everything to her llama, Tinkles."

Rex frowned. "Leaving your fortune to your pet is a relatively new invention from this century. Do we know how that played out? Who was responsible for taking care of the money for the llama?"

I shrugged. "It's getting late. Let's grab some dinner, and tomorrow I'll ask Edna. If she knows about the will, she must've seen it."

"Good idea." Rex started the car.

After a quick bite to eat at Oleo's, Rex got a call from the office and dropped me off at home.

There was a car in my driveway. A black SUV. I only knew of one person who drove that particular car.

"What are you doing here?" I loomed over Riley Andrews, my former boss and brief ex-boyfriend who was sitting on my couch with my traitorous cats in his lap. I slammed the door behind me, causing the beasts to scatter.

He grinned. "Nice to see you too, Wrath."

What was this man doing back in my life? Riley and I had worked together for years—me as a spy, him as my handler. And we'd worked well together. Too well. At one point our relationship had turned romantic.

I wasn't sure why I'd fallen for his charms after years of watching him hit on countless other women. Some were part of the job, others…well…

I should've known better. But espionage was lonely work where you toiled in a foreign country with just one other CIA agent. Eventually that other person, whose tricks you were completely aware of, started looking pretty good.

It didn't help that Riley was attractive, with his wavy blond surfer hair that was a bit too long for regulation and blue eyes that could melt the panties off even the toughest German prison matron. The problem with Riley was, he was a terrible womanizer, pursuing gorgeous women like a starved lion at an all-meat barbecue. He didn't take women seriously. To be honest, he didn't take life seriously.

And when he turned those attentions on me, in spite of what I knew, I was a goner. I'd always thought of it as the stupidest moment of my career. But it was also one of the most passionate. Riley was irresistible, and when he looked at me, I felt like my underwear was on fire.

Unfortunately, it came to an end when I caught him with another woman. Only in the last year did I realize that it had all been a misunderstanding and I didn't really see what I thought I'd seen. Or maybe I wanted out of the hot-and-bothered mess.

That was also about the time Riley started showing up in my life again—turning his charm all the way up to one million and leaving me breathless. He'd admitted that he still had unresolved feelings for me. The question was then, and possibly now, did I feel the same way?

I sat down in the chair opposite him. "Don't tell me... you're working on a case."

After an "issue" with the agency, Riley had transferred to the FBI. I wasn't even sure you could do that. He was stationed in Omaha, a little more than two hours away, and always seemed to find a reason to stop in Who's There, usually by breaking into my house.

"You still have my key?" I held my hand out.

He didn't hand it over. "I'm not working on a case. I wanted to bounce something off of you. I'm thinking of leaving the FBI, moving to Des Moines, and opening a private investigation firm."

He studied my reaction. "I'm guessing by the fact that your mouth is hanging open that you're surprised by this idea."

Somehow, I managed to close my mouth.

"For a moment I thought you said…"

"…that I'm moving into the area to work full-time. Yes, I said that."

A million thoughts went through my head, and I found it tough to compartmentalize them. Emotions wove a crazy quilt through them, ranging from astonishment to confusion to anger.

"Why would you do that?" I finally said. "You're used to big cities and dangerous assignments. You'd be bored out of your mind here."

He rubbed his chin. "Des Moines is a big city—I could live there. And with all the crazy crap that happens around you in a small town like this, I doubt I'd ever be bored."

My heart was hammering a hole in my chest. "You can't be serious."

Riley shrugged. "Maybe I want to get out of this field. Maybe I'm thinking of settling down somewhere. Meeting the right woman, starting a family."

My throat stopped working. I couldn't even swallow. I'd just gotten over my insomniatic anxiety over marrying Rex. I did not need Riley coming along to confuse things, or worse, try to get me back.

"It's not so farfetched." Riley relaxed. "You did it."

I found my voice. "Not because I wanted to! I was forced to retire!"

"You could've joined the FBI, or Homeland Security, or something like that. Lived in DC or New York. Instead, you came here. And you seem reasonably happy."

I narrowed my eyes at those last two words. "I am happy! Besides, this is my hometown—it's natural for me to come back here. You're from LA. Why don't you go 'settle' there?"

He laughed. "Yes, you're so contented that you bite my head off over the least little thing. I can see that's working well for you."

The rage that welled up in my head was matched only by the doubt that I was happy. Something in my expression must've caused some alarm, because he looked worried.

"Look, it's just something I'm exploring. It's not set in stone."

"And your reasons for not moving back to the West Coast?"

Riley toyed with a thread on my couch that wasn't there and said quietly, "There are some things here that I don't think I can find there."

I threw my arms up into the air and screamed. This man could make me insane. I wondered if I should just kill him and be done with it. I could probably hide a body in my basement and get rid of it under nightfall...

Riley got to his feet. "I should go. I have a meeting in the big DM in half an hour." He seemed to be waiting for me to stand up.

I remained where I was. No way was I going to stand up and have him hug me or kiss me or anything dangerous like that.

"Don't call it the big DM," I said. "Nobody does that."

"I'll let myself out." He gave me a wink before he left.

For about forty-five minutes, I sat there, staring at the wall. Philby jumped into the air in front of me, but I barely saw her. All I could think about was how I was going to lose my mind if Riley moved to the area. And if he did...

I was well and truly wubbled.


I had to wait until dusk. That was when the zoo was really empty. Obladi Zoo closed at five, and for a couple of hours the staff would clean stalls and feed the animals. After that there were maybe one or two people there. I could dodge them.

Hauling myself up and over the fence, I pulled out the key I'd had made to the aviary and let myself in. The birds largely ignored me except for a scarlet macaw who said, "There she is again! Go home, Ms. Wrath!"

"What the..."

"Squawk! She's a weirdo!" The bird stuck its tongue out at me.

It took me a moment to figure out it must be because of that kid who always seemed to catch me here. How many times did he say that for the bird to remember it?

Mr. Fancy Pants spotted me right away and stared directly at my bag. Using another key that technically didn't exist (because I'd stolen and copied it on the sly), I let myself in and sat on the log. The king vulture jumped up next to me, his eyes riveted on the bag.

Reaching in very slowly, I pulled out a handful of shortbread Girl Scout Cookies and set them on the branch between us. The bird devoured them. I repeated this process until the entire box was gone.

When he realized the cookie fest was over, he sat up and stared at me with his googly eyes.

"So," I said with as much dignity as I could muster when talking to a vulture, "Riley's thinking of moving here. Well…not *here*, here. But close. And he wants to start a private eye business."

Fancy Pants rolled his eyes.

I nodded. "I know. I can't tell him what to do. But come on! Does he really think I don't see what he's doing here?"

"She never brings *me* cookies!" The macaw pouted.

I made a mental note to find out what kind of cookies the kid liked. Maybe I could bribe him.

"He's coming here to ruin my life," I continued. "Why can't he just leave me alone?"

The last word rang hollow on my tongue. As if I didn't really mean it. Of course I meant it. Riley being within thirty miles of me was a bad idea.

The vulture opened his right wing and started cleaning his feathers.

"He can't do this to me. I've worked too hard to have a normal life here."

Fancy Pants' head jerked up, and he looked me right in the eyes.

"Maybe I should just tell him to go away and not come back."

The bird bobbed his head.

"That's what you think I should do?"

"I like Thin Mints! But she's never even *asked* me…" the macaw screeched.

I ignored him and looked pleadingly at the vulture.

The macaw shrieked, "*Mom!* I cannot believe you went through my stuff! And no, I don't know where those porno magazines came from!"

Clearly the kid had more problems than just me.

"Tell me straight." I leveled a look at Fancy Pants. "How should I handle this?"

The king vulture stretched upward, and after a few bobs of his head, vomited on my lap. He hopped to a higher branch and stuck his head in his wing.

As I left the building, the macaw shouted, "My life sucks!"

I could understand the feeling.


Since I didn't get what I needed from the king vulture, I called the next best thing. No, it wasn't Kelly. Kelly knew both men well and would've lent an ear, but in the end I needed someone impartial.

Susan was waiting for me in her office. I was lucky I got an appointment with her so quickly, but she insisted she'd had a cancellation and it was fine.

"Hi, Merry!" the counselor said as she waved me over and pointed to a chair in front of her desk.

I'd started seeing the woman a month or so ago. Remember that anxiety insomnia I told you I'd had? Well, Kelly had hooked me up with Susan, and I'd had a rather disastrous sleep study. I thought that I was doing better. Apparently, I wasn't.

"How's the insomnia?" Susan asked.

"Much better. This is kind of a different problem with similar elements."

The therapist laughed out loud. "That's quite an explanation. What's going on?"

She knew about Rex and the wedding. What she didn't know was about Riley. It took twenty minutes to fill her in on the whole story. Frankly, I thought it would take an hour. Susan listened carefully, making a note here and there as I went.

As a spy, no matter which side I was on, I had to look at any situation from both sides. That didn't mean my actions were impartial, but at least I had a base to start from. Sadly, I wasn't being impartial at all in what I told Susan.

I let fly with my feelings toward both men, surprising even myself at my candor. But counselors couldn't repeat the things you said to them, so why not? Maybe if I said everything I really thought, I'd start figuring out things myself.

Trouble was, my own feelings surprised me.

"You have unresolved feelings for Riley," Susan summed up. "You love Rex, but Riley is there in the back of your mind."

I thought about this. Susan was great at waiting for me to respond.

"Are you saying I can't build a life with Rex with Riley in the background?"

She answered, "I think that's what you are saying."

"I think I could move on if Riley didn't keep popping into my life."

"Isn't that just postponing dealing with this?"

I shrugged. "It's the easiest way out. If I never had to see Riley again, everything would work out."

Susan shifted in her seat. "Is that how Rex would see it, if he knew what was going on?"

The diamond ring on my finger suddenly felt very heavy. "Are you saying I should talk to Rex?" That was the last thing I wanted to do.

"Not necessarily," the therapist said. "There are three of you in this relationship, and you're leaving one of the major players in the dark."

She had a way of making me feel she wasn't judging me, which I liked. But was she really thinking I was an idiot? Because I was really thinking I was an idiot.

"You're not an idiot," Susan said.

"*You can read minds?*" I gasped.

The therapist shook her head. "Only on weekends." After she saw the look on my face, she laughed. "Sorry. That was a joke."

"Argh! What do I do?"

"Take a deep breath," Susan instructed. "Riley may never even move here. He could've been saying that to get a rise out of you."

I relaxed a little. "That's true."

"You don't know that he will, and you don't know that he's pursuing you."

"And I have Rex. I love Rex—more than I loved Riley," I offered.

She nodded.

"Maybe I got a little hysterical," I said.

"Completely natural. Getting married is a huge step. It's a rare person who doesn't have doubts or questions." She opened her planner. "When do you want to talk again?"

As I walked out to my car, I felt a little foolish. Who blew their stack when an old boyfriend dropped in out of the blue?

Back at home I poured myself a glass of wine and felt sorry for myself. I do not recommend it. Philby seemed to know I was wallowing in self-pity, because after staring at me for five minutes, she walked along the back of the couch and smacked me across the face. Then, her work done, she curled up on my lap and went to sleep.

Why didn't I get a dog? Or a nonjudgmental guinea pig? A goldfish would've been an improvement over this overbearing, know-it-all fur ball who looked like Hitler.

By my second glass of wine, I was feeling a little stupid. Riley turned up out of the blue, and I ran to the therapist. How did that make me look? Like a weak little girl who didn't know what to do with an ex-boyfriend.

Why was he coming here? I'd never once told him that I was interested. But then, Riley loved a challenge. Any woman who didn't fall victim to his charms would find themselves worn down by the handsome and relentless cad.

I knew this. I didn't want this. I hoped Rex understood it. Damn. I had to talk to my fiancé about this. I didn't want him thinking I was the kind of skank who strung two grown men along. That wasn't my thing.

Hell, relationships weren't really my thing before I moved here. Riley and I lasted a whole New York minute. Or rather, a Bogotá minute, which was about thirty-three seconds.

Since I was trying to be honest about this—was I ready to get married? Not because of Riley, but because of me?

On the plus side, Rex and I had been together for two years. Our relationship was on course for moving in together or getting married. And Rex wasn't really the type who wanted to just live together. He wanted to make it official. He was mature and decisive. And when he was ready to make the commitment, he was totally ready. Rex was a grown-up. Riley was the spoiled child.

On the negative side, I'd always been a late bloomer. Whether it was puberty or discovering my independence—it took me twice as long as normal people. I was wary, unsure of what I really wanted out of life.

Up until two years ago, I knew exactly what I wanted—to work for the CIA. But now that I thought of it, I wasn't really independent. I lived wherever the agency told me to. I followed their plan, and everything I ate, every place I slept reflected that.

You have no idea what it's like to go from a situation where all decisions are made for you, to having to suddenly buy a house, shop for groceries, and decide what to do with your day. Or maybe you do. I shouldn't judge.

In fact, I was a bit jealous of Rex's ability to behave like an adult. In my last job I pretended to be an adult, or a man, or once…a transgendered person who was into infantilism (but only that once). It had taken me a year to take down the Dora the Explorer sheets I used as living room drapes and buy real curtains.

Kelly knew this about me. But she was the penultimate grown-up too. Right out of college with her nursing degree, she got married, got a job, and started a family. I ate ravioli out of the can, my favorite food was sugar, and I could barely manage two strange cats. I didn't even get the cats myself—they were thrust upon me during a murder investigation.

No…my not being ready for marriage had nothing to do with Riley. It had everything to do with me. I was the one who needed work.

Whew! Either Susan triggered this introspection, or this $6 wine was better than I thought. I opened a can of ravioli, poured another glass. I had to get my mind off Riley Andrews, and I was pretty sure what would help.

The case had been in suspended animation while I had my pity party. I needed to find out if Margaret really was Peggy. Peggy McMurtry, so I took my glass of wine to my room where I curled up in bed with the diary.

I found it on page fifty-two.

*July 26*

*Dearest Friend, Margaret came over to help me with Tinkles' bath. Since Eustace has moved on, it is nice to have a friendly face to talk to. Margaret is my second cousin—the granddaughter of my grandfather's sister. She has only recently moved here, staying in a boarding house. I did not even know I had a cousin. Grandfather has never mentioned any family. He welcomed her when she arrived with a note from his sister and set her up in a nice boarding house down the street.*

There was a mention, but it was Margaret, not Peggy. That was what threw me. Peggy was a common nickname for Margaret, so this must be her. I kept reading.

*July 30*

*Dearest Friend, Margaret has been a godsend. We spend every moment we can together. She loves Tinkles, and we take him for long walks through the country. This poor girl told me her sad story. It would appear that her mother was ill for some time, and her father had left. Margaret was her mother's caretaker until she had to enter an asylum. That is what brought my cousin to me.*

*. We have become fast friends, as she loves butter too.*

*August 2*

*Dearest Friend, I nearly died today. My cousin and I were walking in the woods, and I lost my footing, nearly falling down into a ravine. My ankle was badly injured, and Margaret ran off for help. Eustace found me and carried me home. He seemed confused when I thanked her for fetching my brother. She was sitting on the porch, drinking lemonade when we arrived at the house, and flew into action, making me comfortable on the settee and waiting on my needs for the rest of the evening. I am fortunate to have such a considerate friend.*

My spy-dy senses tingled. Had Margaret/Peggy sought help? Or had she left Mimi in the woods to die?

# CHAPTER THIRTEEN

————

The next few months of diary entries followed a similar formula. Peggy running out on an errand, leaving Mehitable in a house that mysteriously caught fire. Peggy accidentally putting arsenic in Mimi's tea instead of sugar. Peggy tripping into Mehitable when the girls were standing on the edge of a cliff.

And in each of these scenarios, Mehitable remained innocent of her cousin's attempts to kill her. But had Peggy killed her cousin with an axe? She'd tried to make all these other incidents look like accidents. Did she just lose it one day and kill her flat out? Did she tell the marshal that it was an accident?

Or was Peggy an innocent walking calamity? With no desire to kill her cousin? What would her motive have been? Money? Revenge against her great uncle? Madness? Did she think that she might replace Mimi in the family?

Was she really a relative? Was the letter forged? Was she a con artist? Was she a murderer?

I put the diary down and rubbed my eyes. It was eight in the morning. I'd been reading and rereading these passages all night. I needed some sleep. One thing I'd learned from years of espionage—your mind plays tricks on you when you are sleep deprived. Maybe I could have Rex read the diary and see what he thought.

Setting the book aside, I pulled up the covers and passed out.


My phone was buzzing on the nightstand, forcing me to wake up. It was Kelly.

"Yes?" I asked groggily as I stared at the time. I'd been asleep for four hours.

"I have an idea. Meet me at the park in twenty minutes." My best friend then hung up.

After feeding the cats and a quick shower, I arrived at the park to see my whole troop waiting for me. What was this?

"Did we have a meeting scheduled?" I rubbed my face.

Kelly shook her head. "No. But I was thinking we could use this opportunity to earn our Map Skills patch."

I stared at her. "You woke me up and called twelve sets of parents for this?"

Was I about to murder a woman who beat up a bully for me in third grade?

She rolled her eyes. "It's a good idea."

"Why the Map Skills patch?" I looked at the girls, who were decked out in adventure gear. Lauren was even wearing a pith helmet, and Emily had a walking stick.

"Because of the map we found in your yard," Kelly grinned. "It's a perfect tie-in!"

That was when I knew I was outgunned. And that Kelly must've known about this in advance because she provided each girl with a map of the town and a list of items for a scavenger hunt.

"I thought you said you just came up with this?" I groaned.

"I did." Kelly sniffed. "But I've had these scavenger hunt lists for months."

I stood by as Kelly organized the girls into three groups of four, reviewed the rules, and sent them out of the park and into town.

"You didn't even need me here." I yawned.

"Of course I need you here."

Something was off.

"What's really going on? A surprise playdate? You'll have to do better than that."

Kelly put her hands on her hips. "This isn't that unusual. Last summer you came up with that survival retreat at camp at the last moment. It wasn't easy finding water-purifying pills and camo face makeup at the last minute."

"That was different. That was a course on sudden survival. Like if we all woke up to a zombie apocalypse."

She narrowed her eyes at me. "Well, that explains why you had them make a fence out of pointed sticks."

"Those are practical life skills," I protested.

"And then you had a surprise trip to the army surplus store in the city. You bought them all ghillie suits and knives."

I shrugged. "What's wrong with knives? Boy Scouts have knife skills! Girl Scouts have knives!"

She tapped her foot. "Not the size of machetes. Do you know how hard those were to return?"

"Killjoy," I grumbled.

"Okay," she relented. "I needed something to occupy my time today."

That got my attention. "Why?"

"Because Robert wanted to go golfing for the fifth time this month, leaving me to babysit Finn. I wanted some time off. So I invented this."

My jaw dropped. "That's diabolical."

"I had to get out of the house. I love my daughter, but I need some space now and then."

"Okay."

Kelly's right eyebrow went up. "Okay?"

I nodded. "Okay. Let's make this really fun."

"It is really fun." She shoved the list under my nose. "I've been working on this list for a while, thinking we might do this."

I took it from her. There were ten items ranging from a pinecone to a purple barrette. I'd at least have added something like "make a weapon using things found in nature" or "set up a booby trap using dental floss and four toothpicks." Of course then it wouldn't be a scavenger hunt, but it would be more interesting.

I could use a little fun to blow off some steam. Get my mind off of dead heiresses, llamas, and Ike's axe murder. If we were going to do this…we were going to do this right.

Spy style.

Moments later, hiding in a prickly shrub, Kelly asked, "Why are we following them?"

"To make sure they aren't cheating. And to see how they're going to pull off scoring a piece of twine from somebody."

Kelly glared at me as she picked a bit of greenery out of my hair. "Why do you think that would be difficult?"

I rolled my eyes. "Because no one has twine anymore."

"And this is fun because?" she added.

"Because we never see what they're like on their own," I explained. "Don't you wonder how the girls act when not around us?"

I did. Maybe it was my suspicious spy training or maybe it was because I didn't think these outrageous little girls could possibly be so precocious outside of troop time. Or maybe I was completely mental. I wouldn't rule that out.

"That's why you chose Betty's group," Kelly said in an *aha* tone.

Betty, Lauren, Inez, and Ava were walking from door to door, not too far from my house, asking for twine. Once again, they were turned down.

"What, did you get that list from a magazine from the 1950s?" I whispered. "What would people use twine for these days?"

Kelly grumbled, "I have twine."

I looked at her. "And what do you use it for?"

"Stuff," she said grudgingly.

"What stuff?" I pressed.

Betty was arguing with a little old lady who was insisting that she hadn't had a ball of twine in years, but offered up some fluffy pink yarn. I pointed this out to Kelly, who grumbled. As she folded her arms over her chest, a twig snapped. We froze.

Lauren's head spun about, studying the shrubs we were hiding in from across the street. For a moment I thought she'd spotted us, but she went back to following Betty's argument. The old woman slammed the door, leaving the four girls to retreat to the sidewalk.

"That's going to be the toughest thing on our list," Ava said.

"Maybe we could make our own twine?" Lauren asked.

"Okay." Betty led the girls across the street to where they stopped in front of us. "How do we make twine?"

The four girls studied their cell phones for a minute. Frankly, I was impressed with the idea. I didn't know how twine was made either, but there'd been many a time in the field when I'd had to improvise.

Once, in rural Romania, I'd had to make a gun holster using a piece of tarp and a twist tie. Another time, in Bogotá, I'd had to make a speaker for my cell phone, using a toilet paper tube. And in Marrakech, in order to make a prisoner believe we'd taken him to Siberia, I'd had to make fake snow using a large package of tube socks and a tray of ice cubes.

"I don't think we have time for this," Inez said. "We'll just have to go back without it."

"*We can't go back without it!*" Betty screamed.

I knew it. I knew she talked in italics.

Lauren shrugged. "Why not? If we can't find it, how will the other teams?"

"Maybe Mrs. Albers and Mrs. Wrath don't know what twine looks like?" Ava suggested. "We could substitute it with something else?"

"I've got a pair of handcuffs," Betty said, pulling the manacles out of the back pocket of her shorts.

"I think twine is like rope." Inez shook her head. "Let's find some rope."

The girls took off down the sidewalk, and after a moment we followed them. Following someone was easy. People rarely suspected that they were being watched. Especially if they weren't spies.

Following Girl Scouts, on the other hand, was hard. Every thirty feet or so, Lauren would turn around and look in our direction. Kelly and I became masters of hugging fences and trees at just the right moment.

"Why does Betty have handcuffs?" Kelly hissed during a particularly long hiding session behind a bush.

"I'd be more surprised if she didn't have handcuffs," I responded.

We maintained a half-block distance from the girls as we crossed over into familiar territory—my neighborhood. We were two blocks from my house.

I know this might come as a bit of a surprise, but I don't really know much about my neighborhood. Yes, I used to be a spy, and of course spies have to know the area better than they know their own house. But I didn't.

Exercise like walking or jogging wasn't really my line. And even though I grew up here and could find all the landmarks, I hadn't taken time to look into my own neighborhood. Seemed like sloppy work on my part.

"Hey!" Kelly whispered and pointed to a ranch house that looked like mine. "That's the other address for Ike Murphy's house!"

"How do you know that?" I asked.

"I told Robert that we found what we thought was your body's house. He told me he knew Ike and where he lived."

"My body?" I asked, a little offended.

Kelly nodded. "They're always your body. You find them."

"I don't think that's fair. I didn't even know Ike."

"Well, you found him, so he's your body," Kelly said.

The girls paused in front of the house for a second before climbing the stoop and ringing the doorbell. We waited, knowing no one was home to answer. Eventually, the girls would give up and move on. Then maybe I could talk Kelly into checking it out.

The door swung open, and a middle-aged woman looked from side to side before focusing on the girls.

"Who's that?" Kelly breathed.

I shook my head in surprise. "No idea."

"Maybe she's related?"

I stared at the large, middle-aged redhead who was glowering at the girls. "Edna Lou implied he was her only relative. I got the impression that Ike didn't have family."

Betty asked if the woman had twine. She nodded, shut the door, and returned moments later with a whole ball that she told the girls they could keep. After some fist bumps and shouts of joy, the girls ran off, out of our line of sight.

Kelly and I kept staring at the house. The idea of following the girls was over. In fact, I wasn't sure what surprised me most—that someone was there or that she had twine.

"What should we do?" my best friend asked.

I stood up and stretched. "Go over there, obviously."

Kelly started to follow me. "And do what?"

I grinned. "Find out what's going on. Come on."

We stepped up to the house and rang the doorbell. And waited. And waited. And waited. I rang it again. Nothing happened. No one came to the door.

"Maybe she's in the bathroom?" Kelly offered.

"Or she's avoiding us." I hit the doorbell again.

The woman we'd just seen never answered. The window was covered by drapes, so I made for the long driveway. No car. That was strange. We'd have seen if she'd driven away. I walked back to the garage and peeked in a window. No car in there either.

There was a side door, so I knocked with pretty much the same result. Where had she gone? Had she slipped out the back after the girls left? Why would she do that?

"Can I help you?" An elderly man came out of the house next door and walked over to us.

I put on my most innocent smile. "We were looking for the lady who lives here."

The stooped man looked confused for a moment. In spite of the summer heat, he was wearing a long-sleeved, plaid flannel shirt and a pair of khaki pants.

"I think you have the wrong place. Ike Murphy lived here. And he died recently."

"Oh? I was told that a woman lived here. Middle-aged? Maybe Ike's daughter?"

The man threw back his head and laughed. "Ike? With kids? That's a good one! I can't wait to tell the guys at the café tomorrow. They'll love it."

I pasted on a look of confusion. "He didn't have children? Maybe it was a niece?"

He doubled over with laughter that turned into a severe coughing fit. Kelly, ever the nurse, patted his back and looked him over.

"Nels Larson," the man said between wheezes as he tried to catch his breath. "I've been Ike's neighbor for fifty years. He never married and never had children. In fact, I think his only relative is Edna Lou Murphy. And she never married or had kids either."

So, no niece. Who was that woman we'd seen talking to the girls?

"We must've been mistaken." I said. "You knew Ike? Why is it funny for us to think he had kids?"

"Come on inside," Nels insisted. "I need to take a pill."

"That's very kind of you," Kelly said. "But we don't mean to impose."

I nudged her with my elbow.

"I don't get many visitors," Nels said. "This is the most excitement I've had in weeks. Come in." He turned and walked up the three steps to his side door, and we followed.

The interior of the house was like mine, if I'd been trapped in a time warp from the 1970s. Everything was clean, but worn and outdated. Nels seated us at the kitchen table, and after taking a pill that would send a horse running in the opposite direction, he pulled a pitcher of lemonade from the fridge and poured us each a glass before sitting down to join us.

"You asked why I thought it funny that you thought Ike had family," Nels stated.

I nodded.

"Ike Murphy was a sorry sumbitch who didn't like anyone. No woman ever came near him, except for Edna Lou, his cousin."

"Edna Lou, from the Historical Society," I said.

"Yup." Nels nodded. "That's her. Last of their families, they are." He frowned at his glass of lemonade. "I mean were, in the case of Ike."

I felt even sorrier for Edna Lou. How awful to be alone. I was an only child, and I had more family than she did.

"You knew Ike well?" Kelly asked.

"As well as anyone could. He kept to himself. Never had any interest in hanging out with the guys at the café. Mostly we just drink coffee and gossip."

"Yes," I started. "But living next door to a man for all those years, you must have gotten to know him somewhat."

Nels looked off into the distance, mouth open. He sat that way for a minute. I was afraid he'd slipped into a coma. One where you're sitting in your kitchen, holding a glass of lemonade. Finally he snapped out of it and gave me a look I couldn't decipher.

"Oh, I knew him. He worked at the hardware store all his life. Loved local history. In fact, he and his cousin ran the local group." He took a long drink from his glass. "Talked to himself too. Always mumbled as he worked around the yard."

Kelly and I leaned forward. "What did he talk about?"

"Let's see…" Nels tapped his chin thoughtfully. "Well, usually it was his hatred of the paper boy." He looked at us. "Robby Billingsly." He shook his head. "Nice kid but lousy paper boy. Always tosses mine in my rose bed."

"Is that why Ike didn't like him?" I couldn't bring myself to say "hate." Who hated a kid?

"Nope. He used to say that someday he'd be rich and he'd buy the paper and fire Robby. Well…he *used* to say that."

I picked up the thread and began to pull. "Used to?"

"The other day I heard him mumbling about gold. Told himself he had a couple of gold bars and soon he'd be able to buy this whole town."

I held my breath. This was confirmation that Ike had found the treasure!

"What do you think he was talking about?" Kelly pressed.

"I don't know," Nels said. "But I've always wondered about that story about the missing Peters' fortune."

This was it! "The missing fortune?" I asked. "Isn't that just a story?"

"On no, missy!" He slapped the table, making me jump. "It's real alright! And I think Ike found it."

"Where did he find it?" Kelly asked quickly.

I shot her a look. These things had to be finessed. You couldn't just come right out with the big question.

But Nels seemed happy and eager to impress. "I think he just found it recently. You know, it's funny. But Ike never had much use for modern things. But a couple of days before he was killed, I saw him talking to someone on a cell phone." He sat up straight. "Maybe that's the woman you're looking for! He said, 'You're my pretty, lucky penny!'"

I frowned. "He said that to whoever he was talking to?"

Nels nodded. "I even asked him why he had a cell phone all of a sudden, and he told me he had to talk to his girlfriend and that he was rich."

My cell went off just as I was going to ask for more information. It was Emily.

A voice exploded in my ear. "Mrs. Wrath! You and Mrs. Albers are missing! We're at the park, but you aren't here! *Where are you?*"

I promised that we were on our way. We thanked Nels, and then Kelly and I ran across town to make it to the park before the parents noticed we weren't supervising.

The teams were waiting for us, each with a plastic bag that looked full. Kelly took charge and had each team go through their bag, but I was miles away, wondering who Pretty Lucky Penny was.

She had to be the woman we saw at Ike's house. I'd already decided the woman was still in the house when we knocked. Ike's conversation with her led me to believe her name might actually be Penny. Why else call her "Pretty Lucky Penny"?

A gasp went up beside me, shaking me from my reverie. One of the Kaitlyns was holding up a living, wriggling garter snake.

"The list says *stake*! Like you'd use for a tent!" Kelly shouted as she backed up.

Kelly did not like snakes. In high school we'd been lab buddies. Someone (who shall forever be known as Kevin) had substituted a real, live snake for our real, dead one. When she'd put the scalpel to its skin, the reptile rose up and jumped at her.

I'd never heard her scream so loud then or since. It had also been the first time Kevin had demonstrated the use of more than one brain cell.

Kaitlyn tossed her snake into the grass, and as it slithered away, I saw two other groups let snakes out of their bags. In a way, I was proud. How many little girls didn't mind handling snakes?

None of the first three groups was able to find twine. I thought about lording it over Kelly, but I knew what was coming up as Betty, Lauren, Ava, and Inez stepped forward with their bag.

One by one, the girls did like the others, emptying the contents and holding them up for everyone to see. This group went a bit farther than the others, as they had, in fact, turned everything they found into weapons.

The pinecones leaves, or whatever they're called, were sharpened, making it look like a spiny grenade. We also had a twig sharpened into a kind of spear, a rock that had been chipped into a hatchet head, and a dandelion chain that resembled a garrote.

I wanted to award them extra points for taking the scavenger hunt to the next level. Although I wasn't sure Kelly would like that.

At long last Betty dramatically unveiled the pièce de la résistance—the holy grail—the ball of twine. The other girls gasped appreciatively as Betty fashioned that into a noose.

"Betty," I said once the presentation was over. "Can I talk to your group for a second?"

The girls rolled their eyes at each other but joined me twenty feet away from the others.

"At the house where you got the twine…" I began.

Betty's eyes narrowed. "We didn't buy it. A lady gave it to us."

"I didn't think you…"

"You know that," Lauren said. "Because you were following us."

My mouth shut as I tried to puzzle out an excuse. But then I realized that them knowing we'd seen them would work to my benefit.

"I just wanted to ask you about the woman you got it from. Can you describe her to me?" To be honest, we were across the street at the time and probably missed something.

Ava shrugged. "She was old. Maybe even older than you."

"She wore a dirty T-shirt and shorts," Inez added. "And frizzy red hair."

"She wasn't very nice," Lauren said.

Betty scowled. "She was nice enough to give us a whole ball of twine."

Lauren thought about that. "That's true. But she looked angry that we were there."

Ava nodded. "But she must've lived there because she found the twine really fast."

"Probably trying to get rid of us," Inez said. I ignored this. "Did you see into the house at all?"

The four started talking all at once, and I had to use the Girl Scout quiet sign to silence them. I pointed to Betty.

"It was dark in there, but I saw some furniture turned upside down."

Inez spoke up. "I think she had a gun."

We all looked at the girl.

"It was in the back of her shorts when she turned around."

The other girls thought this was a totally normal and acceptable explanation.

"I didn't think it was her house," Lauren said. "It took her a long time to get the door open. Like she didn't know how the locks worked."

"She knew where the twine was though," Ava repeated.

I thanked the girls and sent them back to the others, who were in the middle of a game of tag. And thought about what I'd just heard. Penny was dirty, and the house was trashed. My guess was she was dirty from trashing it. Penny fiddled with the locks but knew where the twine was. She didn't live there, but was familiar with the place.

Nels overheard Ike say he had a girlfriend and was rich. Which could only mean that Penny was his girlfriend and he'd found the gold. Well, that and because we'd found a gold bar at the Historical Society.

And all of these clues added up to one fact—Penny had just become my top suspect.

# CHAPTER FOURTEEN

———

"Merry?" Mom asked through my phone.

It was a few hours after the scavenger hunt. Rex had to work late, so I'd made a gourmet dinner of canned ravioli and a glass of wine. The wine made it gourmet, naturally.

"Mom! You got my message? With the picture?" I set my fork down and grabbed the copy of the photo of young, not insane Mehitable Peters.

"I did. Why did you send this to me?" she asked.

I scrolled through my messages. I thought I'd texted her, but apparently I just sent the photo.

"It's Mehitable Peters." I stared into the woman's eyes. "Mad Mimi."

There was a moment of silence on the other end. That wasn't too unusual. Mom was working on a huge summer gala fundraiser at the Kennedy Center, and sometimes she was interrupted. I'd gotten used to her having to hit the mute button now and then.

"I'm sorry, kiddo," Mom said. "Are you saying this is the woman who died in an axe accident years ago?"

"Yes." I was surprised she didn't know that. "That's right."

"Why did you send it to me?" Mom sounded genuinely puzzled.

"I was wondering if we were related. Rex thinks it looks a lot like me." That was technically true.

"Now that you say it," Mom said slowly. "I can see that. But I don't think we're related."

"What about on Dad's side of the family?" My heart sank a little. Although why I was disappointed was beyond me.

"Give me a few moments, and I'll call you back." Judith hung up.

This was crazy. I was sure we weren't related. It wasn't that long ago, and Grandma Wrath would've told us if we were. The fact that I looked like Mimi was just a distraction from the real issues of her murder and Ike's.

I traced Mimi's face with my finger. *What happened to you?*

The cell rang, and I snatched it up. "Mom?"

"Your father doesn't know," she said. "But he doesn't think so."

"Does he know his mother's maiden name?" I asked.

I heard her mumbling in the background. "He says his mother's name was McMurtry. Colleen McMurtry."

I sat very still, afraid I hadn't heard correctly. A doorbell rang in the background.

"I have to go, kiddo. The committee has arrived, and we have lots to do."

We said our goodbyes and hung up. Mimi's face stared up at me. She'd died in 1911. Dad was born in 1966. His mother's name was Colleen McMurtry, and Peggy McMurtry was Mimi's long-lost cousin.

Why had I never taken up genealogy? Wait! I remembered seeing an ad for a website. Pulling out my laptop, I got online and found it immediately. After paying with my credit card, I was presented with a little box for my name.

I plugged in my name and birth date, and my parents', including Grandma Adelaide and the name Colleen McMurtry. I didn't know either woman's birth date, but according to the website, I should get a little branch figure when there were hints that would lead me to answers.

Nothing happened. How long did it take to get a branch? Hours? Days? I didn't have that kind of time! Was there a way to hurry things up?

Philby jumped up on the breakfast bar and stared at me while shoving the ravioli can onto the floor with a single swipe. Why did cats do that? Martini behaved herself, but Philby was offended when I put anything on a tabletop. She'd broken two mugs and four plates and littered the floor with silverware, glasses, and in one instance, forty-seven bullets. On that day, she'd pushed one bullet onto the floor. The minute I was up from grabbing it, she'd pushed another one off. This went on, you guessed it, forty-seven times.

I could be a little slow on occasion.

After cleaning up I closed my laptop (which fortunately was too heavy for Philby) and tried to focus on Penny. Who was this woman, and why was she at Ike's house earlier? And why did Ike have two properties? And what was I going to do with that flamingo skull?

An idea popped into my head. Of course! I needed to get into Ike's other house. And by doing so, I could leave the flamingo skull there. That would take the heat off me! I'd just have to hide it out in plain sight but in a spot Rex wouldn't necessarily have looked before. How hard could that be?

Night had fallen. Besides, it would give me some time for the branches to pile up on that ancestry site.

I always enjoyed the breaking and entering part of spy work. It was a lot less painful than physical confrontation, and you never knew what you'd find—which was proven by the bras and wigs at Ike's other house. Maybe this house was weirder with bigger skeletons and full period costumes. Or better yet, a stack of gold bars with a note that told us who killed Mad Mimi and Ike Murphy.

It only took a few minutes to change into a pair of dark capri pants and a dark T-shirt. Throw in a black backpack with a hat inside and a pair of ballet flats, and I might get away with looking somewhat normal to anyone in the vicinity.

I tossed my lockpick set into the bag and threw in a gun. After thinking about it, I added a telescoping baton. No point in firing a shot if I didn't need to. Besides, the baton was new, and I hadn't had a chance to try it out.

It took only a few minutes to get to the house. Nels, next door, had lights on, but in a room on the opposite side of the house from his driveway next to Ike's. Walking around to the alley in back, I found no fence, which was great, but no trees or shrubs or any cover, which was not.

The house and garage were dark, so hopefully Penny wasn't there. She was a big lady, and even though I thought I could take her, it was best to avoid running into her. Hugging the back of the house, I listened for any sign of life inside. After I was satisfied that the house was empty, I pulled out my lockpicks and went to work on the back door.

It took longer than I thought. Ike had a doorknob lock in addition a dead bolt a little further up. They looked new. That would take a while. For years I'd worked in third-world countries where locks didn't exist, but when they did, they were practically antiques.

New locks were trickier. The tumblers inside were harder to move, because they hadn't been used much. Why did Ike install new locks just before he died? Because he'd found Mimi's gold! My heart beat a little faster.

Had someone else noticed the new locks? People of Ike's age stuck to the simple doorknob button. They didn't like change, and those simple locks had worked for them all those years. Why switch now?

If someone had seen the new locks, had that tipped them off that finally Ike had something worth locking up? And what about Penny? My guess was that she knew about the gold. If she was his girlfriend, Ike might have told her.

Or he didn't. Maybe they were more like business partners than a romantic couple. And when he found the gold, he'd decided to cut his younger girlfriend out of the riches.

This was all speculation, I thought, as the last lock popped. I quietly put the picks back in my bag and slipped inside the house. It was hot. Whoever took care of the house after Ike's death must've had the power shut off. But then again, old people didn't always use air conditioning.

The only way to know for certain would be to flick the light switch, but that would alert neighbors to the fact I was there. The last thing I needed was Nels calling the police. No, I could work in the dark.

It took a few minutes for my eyes to adjust, but it was still very dim. The going would be very slow, but if I was patient, I just might find what I was looking for.

What was I looking for? The gold would be nice, and it would make the map and its confusing clues obsolete. It wouldn't solve Mehitable's or Ike's murder. It was obvious that Ike was murdered. And I was convinced that Mimi had been.

Even if I found the gold tonight, I'd still try to solve Mimi's murder. Rex had been busy lately and unable to put much time into it. But I was determined to keep going. It was one investigation he couldn't stop me from looking into, and now with possible family connections, I was becoming obsessed with the case.

And then there was Edna Lou. I felt a pang of pity. I'd definitely solve Mimi's murder for her. And Ike's—if Rex didn't beat me to it. And if we found the gold, it was going to the Historical Society. Not one of the Peters was still alive. They would probably approve.

A twinge of guilt pecked at the back of my throat. There was one thing Edna Lou wasn't going to get—the old Peters House. Her dream of turning it into a museum wasn't going to happen as long as my future sisters-in-law lived and worked there.

Randi and Ronni wouldn't give up that house. It was a perfect business for them, and besides, they'd filled every single inch with dead animals. Once this was over, I could find another way for Edna Lou to use the money.

I could see a little better. I started moving. Again I found myself in a kitchen. Only this one was much different than the one in his other house. The smell of rotting food turned my stomach. The counters and sink were overflowing with dirty dishes, and newspapers piled high on the table.

Turning the light on my cell down, I scanned the headlines, hoping maybe they held clues. They didn't. Just a stack of current newspapers. Was Ike a hoarder? I quickly searched the cupboards and drawers but found very little. Most likely because everything was already piled in the sink.

The dining room was next. Again, stacks of newspapers covered the table and each of the six chairs. He had several copies of the same day. Was he planning to move? There weren't any boxes. Instead, the floor was littered with books—westerns mostly. So Ike was a reader.

I moved into the living room. Every piece of furniture had been upended, like the girls had said. A coffee table had been broken in two, and the couch cushions were torn to pieces, as their foam rubber innards lay all over the floor.

Why didn't Penny tear up the kitchen or dining room? Was she looking for the gold? If so, had she found it? I poked and prodded the cushions but decided if they'd been here, they were now long gone.

The hallway to the bedrooms were littered with broken picture frames. All the pictures were missing. Glass crunched under foot, and I froze. If someone was here, they might have heard that.

Why were the pictures gone? Were they sentimental? Were they of Penny? Maybe Penny didn't want anyone to connect her to Ike. She was holding first place on my suspect list. At last I decided no one had heard me, and I moved on.

The flamingo skull was the first thing to go. I had to plant it somewhere. The map! I wondered if Penny had been looking for the map I'd found taped to the skull? It had been useless. Rex's yard didn't have anything as far as I was concerned.

It seemed to me, if you planted a treasure map in my yard, the treasure wouldn't be a hundred feet away. Was it a fake? Mad Mimi was…well…mad. She could've planted all kinds of maps as red herrings. Or just because Tinkles told her to.

I peeked into the bathroom, but it was completely trashed. The floor was slick with shampoo and soap as their crushed, empty bottles riddled the linoleum. The drawers were also on the floor, the shower curtain had been torn off, and the medicine cabinet had been emptied.

I passed it by and stepped into the first room on the right. This was the main bedroom. To my surprise, it was clean. The bed had even been made. Alarm bells went off in my head. Was Penny living here? She hadn't trashed this room. If she wasn't living here, why make the bed?

There were still two rooms across the hall. Both doors were shut. Was Penny in there? I pulled the telescoping baton from my bag and pulled my hat down a little more over my head to fully cover my short, curly hair.

There was no point in retreating. I had to check out those two rooms. Laying the flamingo skull on the bed, I stepped up to the door opposite me and pressed my ear against it. I couldn't hear anything, but that didn't mean the room was unoccupied.

Very slowly I gripped the doorknob and turned. When I felt the door give way, I stopped. If someone was in there, they might have seen the door move. Once again, I waited. Trickles of perspiration ran down the back of my neck over a field of goose bumps.

No turning back now. I opened the door a crack and looked in.

It was empty. There wasn't so much as a stick of furniture, a pillowcase, or even curtains on the window. I opened the door wide and stepped inside. There was nothing in here. Even the closet had been cleaned out.

This was highly suspicious. The whole house was. Only a couple of rooms had been torn apart. So far one room was filthy, one clean, and one empty. Ike was gone, but there'd been a lot of activity in his house recently.

I stepped back into the hall and listened at the last door. What would I find in here? Wigs? Animal skeletons? A stack of gold bars? I turned the knob and walked in.

In the corner was a dresser covered with mannequin heads wearing wigs. In the middle of the room were the skeletons of small animals. And against the far wall was a small pile of gold bars. Was I psychic? Because that would be awesome. I could anticipate anything my troop threw at me. Literally. Would it work on pets? Philby wouldn't be very happy about that, but it would save me in broken dishes.

I started with the dresser, which was more like a vanity table with a recessed area in the middle where the mirror would pop up. The faces on the heads looked a bit more lifelike than I was comfortable with (I could swear one of them winked at me), and I counted eight.

There was a space behind the vanity, and I crouched behind it, feeling the back of the dresser for something that might be attached and hidden.

*Creeeeeeeeeeeaaaak...*

Uh-oh.

I knew that sound. That was a door opening somewhere. And since no one had been in the house up until now, I'd say it was the front door. Which now closed with a muffled thump. Footsteps stalled in the living room before heading down the hallway toward me.

There wasn't enough room behind the vanity to hide me. And since there was a pile of gold in the room, I'd hazard a guess that this was the direction the other guy was coming. I grabbed one of the mannequin heads and took the wig off. Tearing off my stocking cap, I shoved the wig onto my own head and with the bangs low over my eyes, stuck my head up behind the dip in the vanity and froze.

It wasn't my brightest idea. I'll bet you thought spies always outwitted everyone else, didn't you? Well, it wasn't true. Sometimes we just had to go with whatever was available. And tonight, this was all I could come up with. The bad news was that I was exposed. The good news was that I could see.

Sure enough, the door swung open and a figure entered. It seemed to be a woman. My guess was that Penny was back. The woman didn't turn on the lights, reminding me that she wasn't supposed to be here. I was relieved by that because in a lit room, it would be obvious I wasn't a disembodied head.

The woman's eyes played across the room, scanning me along with the other mannequins. How well did she know these wigs? My heart stopped, and it took all of my strength not to blink.

After what seemed like an hour, but was more like a minute, the woman turned away and I was able to look directly at her. It was Penny alright. Same frizzy hair, same angry, middle-aged scowl. She kicked over the skeletons as she walked over to the stack of gold bars.

I watched as she stuffed the bars into a duffel bag. The gold clinked heavily as she dropped them in. It was clear she thought she was the only one in the house. When she finished, she turned toward the vanity, and I barely had time to resume my glassy-eyed pose before her eyes fell on me. I couldn't see them, but I felt the weight of her stare.

And this time, she didn't look away. What was she doing? I breathed slowly through my nose, eyes staring into space, and hoped she couldn't tell that I wasn't made of plaster.

To my horror, she walked straight over to me. This was it. I tightened my grip on the baton under the dresser and waited. I wished I could look at her, but I was pretty sure that even in the dark, she'd notice a wigged head staring straight at her.

Penny reached out and touched the hair of the wig next to me, while humming a song I didn't know. Crap. This was too close. The baton in my hand was extended. It wouldn't be easy to get out and use right away. I should've brought a stun gun.

Oh wait...I didn't have one anymore. That was because several months ago Philby stunned me with it. I'm still not sure what possessed me to have it on the bed, or to leave it on. But Philby came racing into the bedroom one night and pounced on me, which knocked me down onto the fully charged weapon. As I lay there twitching, she had the most curious look on her face. That was when I'd decided to get rid of it.

Penny was touching all the wigs now while humming "Twinkle, Twinkle, Little Star." Her hand was coming right for me and just about touch the curly red mop, when her cell went off.

She roughly tore the wig off my head, and as I prepared to strike, took it and ran out of the room, while fumbling with the duffel bag of gold bars and her cell. I stayed where I was in case she came back, because I couldn't decide if she'd notice that the head she took the wig off of had hair underneath, or if she'd notice that the head was now gone if I'd ducked down behind the vanity.

"Yes!" I heard her shout as the footsteps moved down the hall. "Yes, I've got them. No, not yet. But I should have the rest soon."

The door closed behind her, and seconds later I heard a car roar off into the distance.

I slowly got to my feet and stretched. Now I had two suspects in Ike's murder and the theft of Mehitable's fortune. Because now it was obvious that Penny wasn't working alone.

There was something on the floor where the gold had been. A card of some sort. I scooped it up and hightailed it out of there. I hit the back alley in minutes and shook out my sweat-soaked curls.

In a few moments I was home. I closed and locked the door behind me, leaning against it with my full weight. Philby trotted into the living room, and when she saw it was me, turned and left. I could swear that she was disappointed.

After a quick shower and putting my lockpicks and everything else away, I sat down on my bed and looked at the card I'd found. In careful cursive, it said,

*Lucky Penny, Tinkles awaits…*

# CHAPTER FIFTEEN

———

Rex was sitting at my breakfast bar the next morning. Wrapped in a bathrobe, I kissed him on the cheek and sat down next to him. He'd brought donuts. I swooned.

He stared at the newspaper he was reading. "We had a report of a break-in at Ike Murphy's house. The one near here. The neighbor, Nels Larson, said a woman was fleeing the front of the house."

Relief washed over me. Penny had gone out the front door. I'd used the back.

"Really? Did you look into it?" I shoved a blueberry donut into my mouth and blinked my eyes at him.

Rex put the paper down. "When we got there, the place was empty." He was looking directly at me.

"We were running a scavenger hunt yesterday, and the girls went to that house. A woman answered and gave them a ball of twine." I kept going so he wouldn't have time to ask. "Nels came out to ask the girls what they were doing…" A lie… "And told us that Ike had a girlfriend."

Rex rubbed his eyes. "Why didn't you tell me?"

I shrugged. "I was so busy with the scavenger hunt, I forgot." He was not going to buy that. "The girls all thought the word *stake* was *snake*, and Kelly freaked out at the sight of three garter snakes. Then Betty's team turned all of their items into weapons. It was a bit nuts."

No matter how well Rex knew my girls, he was always surprised by the things they did. I totally understood. I felt the same way.

I pulled my laptop over and opened it up. "I was here all night. Mom called back on the photo of Mehitable. She didn't think I was related to the Peters but gave me Dad's mother's name and maiden name." I opened the website and logged in. "See? I was doing ancestry stuff."

I looked and gasped. I had several twigs both on Grandma Wrath and Grandma Czrygy's names! With a squeal, I opened the profiles and clicked on Adelaide Wrath first.

"Whoa!" I pointed at the screen. "Grandma was married three times! I did not know that!"

Rex narrowed his eyes at the laptop. "Your dad's mom was a McMurtry?"

I nodded. "I just found that out last night…when I was here…all night…doing this." Philby sat in the corner staring at me. Her eyes said *liar.* "Her name was Colleen McMurtry. Coincidence?"

I left Adelaide's profile and clicked on Dad's mom. The first hint said her parents were Thomas and Cindy McMurtry. I saved that information to the file and sat back to wait for another branch to appear.

"Peggy McMurtry couldn't have been Thomas's mother," Rex explained. "She would've taken her husband's name."

"Maybe she had him out of wedlock?" I grew impatient and clicked back onto Adelaide Wrath's profile.

"That could be true," Rex agreed.

I helped myself to another donut. "It says here that Grandma Wrath was married to a Murphy through her first marriage."

"Small towns." Rex shook his head. "Did they have any children?"

"I doubt it. Mom was an only child. I think she'd know if she had half brothers or sisters running around."

Still, Mom had never told me that Adelaide had been married before. Maybe she didn't know?

"I think we're going to have to wait awhile for more hints," Rex said.

I agreed and closed the laptop. I really wanted to tell him about the gold bars at Ike's house. And I wanted to ask why he hadn't seen them when he searched it. Was it possible that Penny found them yesterday when she was tearing the house apart and left them there?

But telling him this would tip him off that I'd been breaking and entering. I'd have to come up with another way to talk to him about it without incriminating myself.

"Since it's Saturday and I'm free," Rex said with a smile, "I thought we'd nose around Mad Mimi's murder a little more."

"That's a great idea! What are we doing?"

"You mentioned that Edna Lou had the original axe at the Historical Society. Why don't we have a look?"

I got dressed in record time while Rex called Edna Lou and set things up. Twenty minutes later we were in the log cabin, huddled over a long, stained cardboard box that held an axe. The metal head was chipped and starting to rust. The wooden handle looked like it had been worn smooth over more than a century. It seemed solidly connected to the axe-head, and had a little hole at the other end.

"They used to put holes in all the tools to hang them up in barns and such." Edna Lou beamed at the gruesome weapon.

I looked closely at the handle. A few stray fibers were stuck to the hole. That must have been hung up with rope. Other than that, the weapon was clean as a whistle.

"It's been in this box since the murder," Edna said. "It was donated to the Historical Society after the funeral. Someone cleaned off the axe-head. They didn't have forensics back then, but it was pretty obvious that there were traces of blood."

"How did you come by it?" Rex asked. "We found some photos of the crime scene. But you don't need to see them."

The elderly woman answered. "Eustace donated it and a lot of other things after the case was closed. There's nothing else directly connected to the murder."

"I'm so sorry," I said.

Rex got up and patted her shoulder, visibly chastened. "I wasn't thinking."

"No, no." Edna blew her nose. "It's okay. Ike and I always wanted to solve this. He would've been excited to see the photos."

Rex picked up his keys. "I'll go get some coffee for everyone."

"Good idea," I mumbled and sat down beside the woman.

"Ike was a good man." She sniffed. "And the only family I had. We were very close."

A thought occurred. "Did he have anyone else in his life? Like a girlfriend or a buddy?"

She shook her head. "No. He kept to himself. Well, he had that neighbor, Nels Larson, who looked in on him from time to time. But Ike wasn't terribly social."

I guess Edna Lou didn't know her cousin as well as she thought she did. How could I tell her about Penny without giving too much away?

An idea popped into my head. "Rex said when they talked to Ike's neighbor, Nels, he said Ike had a girlfriend."

Edna Lou looked at me curiously. I should've waited until Rex was here to spring that on her. Now when Rex came back, I'd have to find a way to update him without tipping her off.

"Ike never dated. Not even in school." She looked around to see if anyone was listening. Which was weird because we were in a cabin made of two-foot-wide logs. "He was, well, delicate."

"Delicate?" I asked. "What do you mean?"

The woman sighed. "I suppose it doesn't matter now. It was a family secret. But Ike liked to dress as a woman."

That explained the wigs and women's clothing.

"He had another house—over by the zoo—where he kept everything. He was very afraid of his secret getting out."

I put my hand on her arm. "That's not so unusual. I mean, it probably was then, but now it's just a lifestyle choice."

Edna nodded. "I know. But he thought it was a secret. He didn't even realize that I knew. Poor dear."

I pressed the issue. "But that doesn't mean he didn't have a girlfriend."

Rex walked in, and Edna excused herself to the bathroom. Which gave me a chance to fill him in on the conversation so far.

"Merry," he said quietly, "you aren't supposed to be investigating Ike's murder. We're here about Mad Mimi."

"I know that. Can I help it if she brought all of this up?" Okay, that was a lie. Still, he didn't need to know that. Okay, he probably guessed.

"I'm so sorry about that," Edna returned, looking a little less fragile. "Can we talk about Mehitable? I'm really not ready to talk about…about my cousin."

"Absolutely," Rex said quickly.

"May I see that photos you mentioned?" she asked. "I'm alright, really."

She really was a trooper.

This case was a passion for her. What would she do once it was solved? I thought about the museum idea. I'd have to find a place for her. Maybe the old Peters lumber mill? It was empty. Up until recently it was a hall you could reserve for special occasions, but it went out of business. Yes. That would be better than evicting Randi and Ronni.

"I can't believe I'm looking at the murder scene," Edna gasped. She squinted at the picture and then got up and grabbed a huge lamp with a magnifying glass on it.

"I use this when I need a closer look," she said as she plugged it in and turned it on. After a few minutes, she looked up. "There's another picture stuck to this one."

Another photo? How had we missed that? We watched in awe, as Edna Lou carefully peeled one photo off of the back of the other. This one was a close-up of Mehitable.

"This wasn't taken at the same time as the other one." Edna tapped the picture.

Rex and I looked at each other.

"See?" She pointed at the close-up and the long shot. "This one was taken during daylight." She pointed at the long shot. "But this was in the evening. Notice the shadows?"

She was right. "How did we not notice this?"

Rex just shook his head. "And I'm a detective."

"Where did you find these?" Edna asked.

I wasn't ready to tell her about my connection to the twins, so I blurted out the only thing I could think of. "Sheriff Carnack found them in some old case files."

That seemed to work.

"Mehitable was fascinated by photography. Did you know she took the picture of herself in the clown suit? As fragile as her mind was, she was very mechanical. Rigged up a camera and took it herself." Edna nodded as if we already knew this.

I was going to have to talk to the woman about leaving info like this out. But then at her age, she probably thought she'd told us already.

She looked around her and finally pulled out a notebook. "I'll have to find the record, but Eustace told the police that she'd become quite paranoid in her last years. Rigged cameras up in every room on the ground floor, using tripwires so she could document any burglaries." She frowned. "Not that there were any back then. Not in this town."

All of this was new information. Information I wished she'd told us earlier.

"Of course, he dismantled all of her booby traps when he took possession of the house," she said, as if that explained it.

Rex and I stared meaningfully at each other. I wasn't sure what we were saying, but I was convinced the words *forgetful* and *bizarre* were part of that conversation. While Edna examined the close-up photo, I decided that as a couple, we were going to have to come up with a secret, silent way of communicating with each other.

Riley and I had done that, I thought with a wince. If one of us was in danger, even at something seemingly benign like a gala at an embassy, we scratched our right ear. If I thought it was time to leave, I tapped my left foot. If he wanted to leave with that hot blonde from reception, he bit his lower lip. Why on earth did I think we'd had a future together?

"I think I'm seeing things." She waved us over. "It looks like there's a reflection in that spoon."

Rex and I crowded around her. Sure enough, Mehitable had a spoon she wore on a string around her neck. And to our shock, it looked like the shadow of a person's reflection in the bowl of the spoon!

I cried out, "That could be her killer!"

Rex stared at the image. "It's definitely a person, but really just a shadow. I might be able to take this to a friend at the Iowa State Police though…for enhancement."

Edna's jaw dropped. "We've solved it? We've solved Mehitable's murder?"

She threw her arms around me. This was exciting. We were so close to finding out who killed Mad Mimi.

"Now we just have to find the fortune and create the museum!"

I stopped jumping. "I have an idea for that. How about the old Peters lumber mill?"

Edna's face fell, and it was devastating. "Oh no, dear. It has to be the house. In Villisca, they give tours in the house. We need to do that to put Who's There on the map!"

I turned very slowly to look at Rex. It was hard to read his face.

"Besides," Edna continued, oblivious to the strange silence in the room. "Now that you've made that generous donation, I can hire a lawyer to get the house."

An awkward silence hung heavy in the air like a wet wool blanket over your head in July. Only this wet wool blanket had embroidery on it that told my fiancé I was financing the future eviction of his sisters. I hoped he didn't notice. And if he did, it wasn't like I was funding state-sponsored terrorists. Oh, wait. I did once. But it wasn't my fault. How was I supposed to know that little Siobhan O'Reilly was collecting for the IRA? She told me it was to save baby loggerhead turtles in Belfast.

Edna busied herself with a notepad, jotting things down. The look on Rex's face was interesting. Bad interesting.

"Merry," Rex said finally, "can I see you outside for a moment?" He looked at Edna Lou. "Do you mind if I borrow her, Miss Murphy?"

Edna Lou nodded. "Of course, Detective! I have so much to do! Take your time!"

Rex and I stepped outside.

"You're financially supporting her in her bid to evict my sisters?" He didn't sound all that mad. Maybe because he thought the old lady was confused and just wanted clarification.

"Um…sorta?" I gave him a weak grin. "I just gave her a donation the first time I met her, and later she told me that she was planning to fight your sisters for their house. I had no idea, I swear!"

He sighed. "I believe you. I really do. But it will be hard to explain to the twins. Especially Ronni."

I slumped. "I know. That's why I was hoping the lumber mill would work."

After a beat, he wrapped his arms around me. "Look, I'm going to scan these and email them to my friend in Des Moines. You stay here with Edna and see if you can find anything more out about Mimi. She might remember other things she hasn't told us. I'll be back in an hour, and we can go talk to my sisters together."

I brightened. "Really?"

He nodded. "Of course. Besides, Ronni's likely to come after you with a dead animal. It would be good for you to have armed backup." Rex kissed me and fled to his car.

Great. I went back inside.

"Edna…" Something was bothering me. "If the two pictures were taken at different times of the day, why do you think the secret photo ended up in the police report with the photo taken at the scene of the crime?"

The woman stopped writing. "I have no idea. Maybe Eustace found the camera after the marshal left and gave him the film?"

"Maybe…" I thought.

Maybe Eustace really had killed his sister. Maybe the marshal didn't want that to get out. I'd been thinking that Peggy McMurtry was the main suspect, but now Mad Mimi's brother was creeping into the picture. Literally.

"I've been all through her diary." I sat down at the table. "There isn't much in there about her social circle, except for a cousin named Peggy. Do you know about her?"

Edna nodded, still writing. "Of course. Peggy was her second cousin on her grandmother Euphemia's side."

Of course. Clearly the elderly lady thought she'd told me this already.

"What's Peggy's story?"

Edna paused and looked up. "She was sent to Iowa from New Hampshire to live with the Peters. I've seen something somewhere that she got into trouble, the poor girl."

"Did that mean she'd gotten pregnant?" I blurted out.

"That's right. But she didn't bring up the baby. There's no record of him until the 1920s, when it was rumored he moved to town." She went back to work as if this conversation was over.

"But in the diary, Mehitable said Peggy's father died and her mother was in an asylum—that's why she was here."

"It's hard to understand," she said, "why that story would be considered a better one than Peggy being in trouble. But there you have it. From what I'd seen in other papers, Peggy's parents were fine. They just didn't want her around."

That was sad. Poor Peggy! How awful it would be if she couldn't see her baby until he was an adult and moved here.

Thomas McMurtry! My great-grandfather! Was it possible that he was Peggy's son? That would explain why I looked like Mehitable. It was a long shot. And when I got home, I'd have to check the website.

This was exciting! I might have a connection to a murder we might have just solved!

"I've been thinking about your map." Edna put her pen down. "Now that we are on the cusp of figuring out who killed her, we should try to solve the mystery of the hidden treasure."

"Good idea," I said.

Personally, I was beginning to think the map was worthless. Found in my yard with very little to go on but some initials and a drawing of a llama, maybe Mimi was just showing how crazy she really was. After all, Ike had found the gold already. Granted, I'd only seen a couple of the bars in person. But that meant the map didn't matter anymore. But how was I going to tell this sweet woman that her cousin had found the money and was going to run off with some woman, leaving her twisting in the wind?

Penny was the key to this. I needed to find her. And I had no idea how to do that.

# CHAPTER SIXTEEN

———

Rex returned an hour later. His buddy at the state police had thought he could help but wasn't sure we'd have much more than a shadow in the image when enhanced. Edna and I were going through some old newspaper clippings on the Peters family.

"I think it's really strange that there are no photos of Eustace and Mehitable's mother." I set some articles aside and rubbed my eyes.

Edna nodded. "It's almost as if they erased her existence. That wasn't too uncommon. Most Americans don't even know anything about their grandparents. Let me ask you, what do you know about yours?"

I shrugged. "Very little. Out of my four grandparents, I only knew Grandma Wrath." I decided not to tell Edna about my possible connection to the McMurtrys. My first priority was solving this case.

"Ms. Murphy," Rex asked.

"Oh! Edna, please!" She blushed adorably.

"Edna"—he seemed uncomfortable using her first name—"can I see the axe again?"

She handed him the box and a pair of cotton gloves. He put these on without question and very gingerly studied the weapon.

Edna Lou pulled out a laptop and began typing. Maybe it was taking too long to write her notes out in longhand.

Penny filled my thoughts. Sooner or later I'd have to tell Rex what I knew. That I'd been in Ike's house and had seen the gold bars. He wasn't going to be happy, but I couldn't see how this investigation was going to move forward without this information.

The risk was that he would be upset with me. But giving him a solid suspect far outweighed that. Didn't it? I was pretty sure Penny was the killer. She'd been talking to someone on the phone the previous night. That was her accomplice.

Probably a man closer to her age. Why else would a fifty-something woman be dating an eighty-something man. She had to be a grifter. The woman must have met Ike, heard him bragging about looking for the treasure, and worked him like a puppet on a string.

Was there a way I could have Rex find her with the gold? Preferably without him knowing I had prior knowledge? That was an idea. But I had to find Penny first. And I wasn't even convinced that was her name.

Nels said Ike had had a cell phone. Was he on social media too? I pulled out my cell and scrolled through Facebook. I doubted he was on anything else. Old people, including my own parents, were on that site these days. Even *I* had an account. I didn't set it up—the girls did it for me. It took me a week to get around to signing in. That was when I'd discovered that they'd created the page for Merry Christmas Princess Poop Pants. I'd since changed it.

I wasn't sure what he looked like, so I typed his name and *Who's There*. Rex was still studying the weapon, and whatever Edna was doing made her grin from ear to ear. Rex couldn't be angry with me for looking up Ike. And if I found him and pictures of Penny, that was how I could implicate her.

Eventually I'd have to confess. But I was a bit of a coward. We were having so much fun looking into Mad Mimi's murder and treasure that I didn't want to ruin it.

There had to be thirty Ike Murphys—fifteen in Iowa alone—and none specifically from Who's There. It took me a few minutes to rule out seven who had full heads of hair...real hair and not wigs.

Eight Ike Murphys. All of them were old and balding. I'd have to go through their profiles very carefully to rule them out. I knocked out five right away because they had pictures of themselves in front of their town water towers.

If you want to know where you are in Iowa, look up toward the sky for the water tower. Every town had one. There were no exceptions. Who's There had a tower that looked like a golf ball on a giant tee. I'd seen towers that looked like coffeepots, giant bowls, and even one in the eastern half of the state that resembled a rutabaga.

The last three Ikes had very few photos and almost no information about themselves. I scoured their timelines but came up empty. And all this time I knew that the one I was looking for might not even have been on social media.

Rex broke the silence. "Edna, may I take these fibers from the axe handle in to our forensics lab? I have a friend there who might have some time on his hands."

Another friend. It was good my fiancé was so well-connected that he…

Friends! Why didn't I think of that before? I barely heard Edna consent. Each of the three Ikes had a few friends listed. The first one didn't have anyone I recognized, but I checked to see if any of them were from Who's There and drew a complete blank.

I repeated this process with the second Ike, all the while chastising myself for not thinking of this before. Nope, this one must live in the northwest corner of the state. I braced myself to come up empty-handed on the last Ike.

Bingo! This Ike Murphy had two friends I recognized…Nels Larson and Penny. Only her name wasn't Penny. It was Penelope May. I guess you could derive Penny from Penelope. It was her alright. Skinny old Ike had his arm around the very same frizzy-haired woman I'd "met" the night before. It was her. No doubt about it.

I scrolled through Penelope's profile. She was from Bladdersly. Of course, she was. A receptionist at a dental office, Penelope May liked country music, travel, and money. She'd actually listed that on her profile.

She had no pictures of Ike on her page. Not one. Well, I guess if I was going to kill and betray someone, I wouldn't have photos of him either.

Now I just had to show this to Rex. That paired with what I'd told him about my conversation with Nels should be enough for him to look into it.

Edna laughed, reminding me that this was sensitive information. I didn't want to upset her, so I could show Rex later. I just needed an excuse to leave...

My cell buzzed with a text from Randi.

"Rex?" I tapped him on the shoulder. "We have to run. Your, um, sister wants to see us about the wedding."

He stood up and helped me to my feet. "I'm sorry we have to leave, Edna."

Good man for not ratting me out.

The woman looked up from her laptop. "Oh? Of course! Where are my manners! I've been sending emails and lost track of the time. You two run along!"

We made it to the car before I thanked him for the smooth exit.

"It was excellent timing. I want to run this axe by the station. As much as I hate lying to Miss Murphy, it was time to go."

I stared at him. "I wasn't lying. Randi really does want to see us. Now."

He slumped a little as he turned the key in the ignition. "Oh well. I'll get another chance to look at the dining room at least."

\* \* \*

We walked in the front door. Ronni, not Randi, was waiting for us. As I turned to look for the absent twin, she smacked me in the head with a dead swan.

"Hey!" Rex got between us. "What's wrong with you?"

Ronni glared at me as if her brother weren't there. "You traitor! You're helping that psycho steal our house!" She stormed off before I could process her accusation.

Rex chased after her, threatening to arrest her, but now I knew what Edna had been doing on her laptop. She'd contacted the Ferguson twins. And she'd told them about my donation.

I was so screwed.

"Merry!" Randi entered the room, full of her usual excitement.

"Randi, I'm so sorry about Edna Lou Murphy!" I said quickly. "It was a total misunderstanding! I would never..."

Randi waved me off with a smile. "Oh, that? *I'm* not worried about her. She has no case whatsoever. It's Ronni you should worry about."

I rubbed my head, feeling a lump form.

"Really, I donated some money to the historical society, and then she told me what she was using it for," I insisted.

"It's fine," Randi said. "That woman has been harassing us for over a month now. Somehow she got it in her head that the previous owner had no right to sell it to us. She claims she's a descendant of the family who built this house and..."

I didn't hear one more word. Pieces of a puzzle I didn't even know I was working on began to fall into place. Somewhere along the line, Edna Lou and Ike's family changed their name from McMurtry to Murphy. Probably because it was easier to pronounce. It happened all the time, except with my father's family who kept Czrygy because there weren't any letters to take out to make an unpronounceable name with no vowels easier.

Edna Lou was a descendant of Peggy McMurtry. How had I missed this? That explained her obsession with the case...her love of local history and genealogy. I wondered why she hadn't told me. I wouldn't have cared if she had a legitimate connection.

People like my grandmother often kept personal information like that to themselves. Adelaide Wrath wouldn't give out any personal information to the census workers who came around every ten years because she was convinced the government would abuse it. So she gave them different numbers every ten years. Why they didn't notice that the household went from twelve to one to seventeen over the course of three decades was beyond me.

Maybe Edna was afraid of what I'd think. Maybe she was embarrassed about her lineage coming from an unwed mother. Whatever the reason, the woman barely knew me. Why would she trust me with such a secret?

It took me a moment to realize Rex was standing next to me, holding what appeared to be a bouquet of prairie dogs. The look on his face said it all as Randi bubbled away about how lovely it would look as I carried it down the aisle.

"Oh! Wow!" I joined the conversation.

"Here!" She took it from Rex and shoved it into my hands.

The marmots were all wearing little green and white tuxedos (the craftsmanship was amazing). I had to hand it to her—she kept with the theme. The only problem with this idea was that I was holding a forty-pound bouquet of dead rodents.

"I'll have to see if this will go with my dress..." I managed.

"Take it with you...you can take it to your final fitting."

I was pretty sure there wasn't a safe spot in my house for it. Philby could get to almost anything through willpower and sheer tenacity. She'd see this as a giant, collective chew toy. Hey, wait...that wasn't a bad idea...

"*Is the traitor still out there?*" Ronni shouted from another room.

Rex turned to me. "I told her if she came into the same room as you, I'd arrest her for assault."

Randi's smile faded. "Did something happen?"

Rex turned to his sister. "Ronni assaulted Merry with a swan."

I couldn't help it. I burst out laughing. The giggles took over in wave after wave as I finally doubled over with hysterical laughter. Tears poured down my cheeks, and after a few minutes I was gulping for air.

Randi leaned close to her brother. "Is she alright?"

Rex sighed. "A little brain damaged from the incident, but I think she'll pull through."

Ronni screamed from her hiding place, "*She'd better quit laughing, or I'm bringing out a heron!*"

Randi followed us out, apologizing the whole way. I could barely breathe, I was laughing so hard. When Rex got me into the car, he handed me the marmot bouquet, and I lost it again. He drove back to my house as I calmed down.

I was still giggling as Rex made us grilled cheese sandwiches. Philby jumped up onto the breakfast bar and gave me a curious look. She was distracted by the prairie dogs and began chewing on one of them.

"Stop that." I took the taxidermied thing away from her and put it on the fridge. It was a temporary hiding place because if Philby wanted something bad enough, she was going to get it no matter what.

"Are you okay?" Rex suppressed a grin as he handed me a glass of iced tea.

I gulped it down. "Sorry. I don't know what came over me."

"Oh yes you do." He leaned over and inspected a bruise that I felt forming where my forehead met my hairline. "I'm sorry about Ronni."

I took a deep breath and pushed his hand away. "It's okay. Seriously. It's okay."

After gulping down another glass of tea and devouring three grilled cheese sandwiches, my head stopped swimming and my thoughts began to coagulate.

"Sorry I'm so weird," I apologized.

Rex looked surprised. "You're not weird."

"I'm totally weird. I just spent half an hour in hysterics for no reason."

"I'd hardly say you had no reason. Between the swan and marmots, I think you handled yourself quite well."

I looked at him. "Why are you so great to me when I'm obviously insane?"

Rex pulled me toward him and kissed my bruised head. "Merry, my family is off-the-charts insane. You're the most normal person I know."

I hadn't thought about that. I was normal compared to his family and his ex-girlfriend, the psycho known as Juliette Dowd. And yet, I was still not as normal as Kelly or my parents. Rex was a keeper.

And then, I remembered all the things I'd been planning on telling him about the case.

"Edna is a descendant of Peggy McMurtry, and I found Ike's girlfriend, Penny, the one Nels talked about, only her name is Penelope May and she lives in Bladdersly!"

Rex took my stream of consciousness outburst in stride, considering the words carefully. I left out the part where I'd broken into Ike's house and Penny had torn the hair off my head.

"Do you think that Edna's ancestry is important?" he asked.

"I think it explains why your sisters' place is so important to her. But I don't think it has any other connection."

"She might be related to you, you know," he said.

I reached for my laptop, but froze. There was more to talk about first.

"I think Penelope is your main suspect." I pulled up Facebook.

"Why?"

"I told you that Nels said Ike had a girlfriend and claimed he was rich. Then Ike shows up dead and Penelope is handing out twine to the girls during the scavenger hunt."

He rubbed his chin. "She might just have been cleaning out his things. That's normal after a death in the family."

"Yes, but Edna didn't even know Penelope existed. She knew her cousin better than anyone!"

"Apparently not."

I thought about this. "He didn't tell Edna on purpose. I think he found the treasure and was going to run off with this woman  He wasn't going to tell his only family member. And if I'm right about her being a McMurtry, then he was too. They worked together at the Historical Society. They had the same motivation."

I showed him Ike Murphy's page, connected to Penelope through his friends list, and went to her page.

"It has to be her," I said finally.

Rex put the dishes in the sink and washed them. He was thinking about what I'd said. I hoped he was agreeing with me instead of trying to read through the lines to find out what I was leaving out.

He laid the dish towel on the counter. "Okay. I'll go see her. Tonight."

"Can I go with?"

"No. You've had a concussion. Stay here, and I'll fill you in when I get back." He kissed me on the lips this time and then left.

I flopped onto the couch, convinced I'd done the right thing. Rex would find out who Penelope really was and maybe even find the gold. I wouldn't have to admit anything. Which was good because I was marrying this man and it wasn't good to go into a relationship with secrets.

Riley appeared inside my head, and I hit him with an imaginary swan. He politely went away. That was one problem I wasn't going to deal with anytime soon.

And soon, we would have the results from the photo with the image of Mad Mimi's murder. Rex would have the woman who killed Ike in custody. That should hopefully lead to the treasure.

Everything was wrapped up. Or would be. I pulled the map out and looked at it again, comparing it to the one I'd found at Ike's first house. The paper was old, but was it one hundred years old? And why were there two?

What was Eustace's involvement in this whole thing? All we knew was that he seemed okay with Mehitable's inheritance, until he couldn't find it, after which he went back to his farm and lived a normal life.

And then there was Peggy McMurtry. The mysterious cousin who'd lied to the Peters when she'd shown up on their doorstep. But maybe that wasn't a sign that she could've murdered Mehitable. What would her motivation have been? To get the house? To get the inheritance? Why would she think that Mad Mimi wouldn't give it to her only brother? We still didn't know why his grandparents cut Eustace out of the will, but maybe Peggy knew and the reason was a deal breaker.

We didn't have enough information. Eustace and Peggy were my favorite suspects, but Eustace was slipping to second place. He didn't really seem to need the money. But a single mother kicked out of her own family? She would.

And what about Mehitable setting up cameras with trip wires? Well, she was mentally unstable. But was she also worried that someone might try something? She didn't seem suspicious of anyone.

At this point in the mystery of a century-old cold case, there wasn't anyone left to interview. We had the diary, but that was it.

The diary...maybe there was something I missed. I ran to my bedroom and plucked it from the nightstand. I'd read the thing over and over. But something told me to read it again. Page by page, I scoured the book, and a couple of hours later I had nothing.

No mention of Mehitable's worries, fortune, or anything new about Peggy. I set the book on the coffee table, but it fell off. This wasn't news—it was one of those do-it-yourself numbers from IKEA that I'd butchered in an attempt to put it together. You couldn't balance a cup of coffee on it, but I hadn't gotten around to replacing it yet.

I reached for the book and noticed something I hadn't seen before. The diary had fallen open to the inside cover. And unless my eyes deceived me, there was a small cut where the leather met the cardboard backing.

I held it up to the light. It was a slit. Purposefully made. And a tiny corner of paper stuck out of it. How had I missed this? I ran to the bathroom and grabbed a pair of tweezers. At the breakfast bar I carefully grasped the corner of paper and slowly wiggled it out of the cover.

After unfolding it, I examined the folded square comprised of several sheets of very thin parchment paper. It was Mehitable's handwriting.

*May 3, 1910*

*All is not as it seems. My grandparents have passed. My cousin remains but has asked about my inheritance many times. She has also moved into my home. I did invite her at first, but she spends all night long roaming the halls, tapping on the walls, and searching in closets. She says we have rats, but I've never seen one. I have seen a six-foot-tall purple cat who likes to stay in our other guest room, but she doesn't seem to mind him.*

*Eustace has offered to send her packing, but it would be terribly lonely here without her. I have moved Tinkles into the house, which vexes my cousin but makes the giant purple cat happy. I am not sure what to do.*

*August 5, 1910*
*Everyone believes me to be mad. I do not think that I am, but then, I did spend the last three weeks dressed as a clown. I am becoming quite suspicious of my cousin . She had words with Eustace yesterday when he suggested that she go back East.*

*Tinkles has been naughty. He has started to chew on furniture, clothing, rugs, anything he can find. Peggy wishes to punish him, but I have stopped her, threatening to evict her if she did any such thing. I suspect the purple cat is behind this.*

*October 6, 1910*
*Peggy is away on holiday, and I am happy. When she returns, I will work with her to make a timeline for her departure. Eustace has been such a blessing. He is even storing my fortune for me on his farm. Tinkles is behaving himself as well. Unfortunately the purple cat has brought home a drunken unicorn who is sleeping off his bender in the attic.*

*January 7, 1911*
*Christmas was lovely. Peggy seems to be penitent and in my good graces as of late. I am once again happy for her companionship. We spend our days making paper dolls, rearranging the books in the library according to color, and sewing costumes. She has embraced my interests, and tomorrow we will have lard sandwiches. The unicorn and cat have disappeared. Maybe they went home for the holidays.*

*March 8, 1911*
*I am so very low. Eustace has been watching over my fortune at the farm—an agreement we had in secret. But Peggy has discovered the truth. I fear Tinkles has informed her. I must be prepared for whatever comes.*

*Tinkles is a naughty llama. I caught him writing to President Taft again. Tinkles seems to think we need to get involved in Nicaragua. But then, he is from South America, so I won't question his politics*

*June 19, 1911*
*Food keeps disappearing from the larder! It has*
*happened three times now. Peggy has gone out East, so we know*
*that it is not her. Tinkles has a new idea (although I suspect it is*
*really from the purple cat). We will set up traps to catch him!*
*Watered the roses with tomato juice—as per their request.*

*June 21, 1911*
*Again with the thievery! Tinkles and I have set cameras*
*in the dining room and kitchen! Now when the thief sets off a*
*tripwire, the cameras will take pictures! We will send the film*
*away, and voilà! In three months we will receive prints and know*
*the identity of the bandit! The flowers have decided they would*
*rather have oatmeal than tomato juice. I wish they would make*
*up their minds! You really can't trust roses.*

*June 25, 1911*
*Peggy will be back soon. I do not know when because*
*Tinkles ate the calendar I wrote it on. The camera has not gone*
*off, and so I have an idea for new traps. The flowers have lied to*
*me. Oatmeal is not helping them. I will try burying limes in the*
*garden. That should do the trick.*

*June 27, 1911*
*Eustace stopped by to visit. He seemed alarmed by my*
*security measures. I am sure he agrees that this is the right*
*course of action! Tinkles has eaten the flowers and the limes. He*
*says it is to punish them. I suspect he put the flowers up to all of*
*these requests, knowing he was going to eat them. President Taft*
*has named the purple cat to be his ambassador to Nicaragua.*
*Tinkles is pleased.*

*June 29, 1911*
*Someone is in the house.*

Huh. I kind of related to these passages. Not that I was
hallucinating like Mad Mimi did, but every now and then, I did

feel like Philby was plotting against me. But maybe that was just par for the course when you owned a cat.

It was obvious that Mehitable's last words predicted her murder that same day. And I was pretty sure I knew who killed her.

# CHAPTER SEVENTEEN

———

"What do you mean, the cousin did it?" Rex joined me in the morning for breakfast.

I poured us each a glass of milk. "It's obvious from her secret diary pages."

"What secret diary pages?"

"Hold up, not until you tell me about Penelope. What happened?"

Rex handed me another chocolate chip donut. "We couldn't find her. We went to her house, her workplace, asked the neighbors and her coworkers. No one has seen her in a few days."

"Does she have family in Bladdersly?" And then I snickered, as I sometimes did, when I thought of the name Bladdersly.

Rex cocked his head to one side. "We can't find anyone. Her neighbors and coworkers barely know her, but they all agree that she's unfriendly."

Philby came over and tried to drink my milk out of the cup. I shoved her aside. She did not look happy. "Has she lived there long?"

"No. Just moved there in the last year. Her boss gave us her application—none of the references are real. He told us to tell her not to come back."

"What do you think?" I asked. After all, he was the professional here.

"I think she's a prime suspect. If she did kill Ike and find the fortune, she's long gone by now. I've put out an APB on her as a person of interest."

As I slid Rex the secret pages, I thought about the few gold bars I'd seen Penny pick up in Ike's house. Was that it, besides the gold bar we found where Ike's body had been in the cabin? That could not be the entire treasure. And I think Penelope knew it. I had a feeling she was still around.

"So the gold was at Eustace's farm?" Rex frowned at the pages. "Maybe it's still there?"

"Or here. Our lots are part of Eustace's farm. The map was on my lot. The treasure may still be here."

"I don't know. These houses were built in the '50s. If there was a treasure here, it would've been dug up by the builders."

He had a point. Did some lucky construction worker hit it rich and keep it secret? We might never know.

Rex's cell rang. It did that. All the time.

"Come with me," he said as he grabbed his keys. "Edna Lou has been attacked."

His first mistake was letting me drive, because his car, it turned out, was low on gas. It would take five minutes to get to town. I made it in three. I wasn't sure Rex appreciated my driving skills. Especially when I took that shortcut through a funeral home parking lot and pharmacy drive-thru.

"You do know that's illegal, don't you?" my fiancé asked. "You're not supposed to use things like that as thoroughfares.

I pretended not to hear him as I screeched to a stop on Main Street.

Edna had been found outside of Ferguson Taxidermy—*Where Your Pet Lives On Forever!* Randi was sitting with the woman on a bench, patting her hand.

"What happened?" I asked as I slammed the car door and ran over.

Edna Lou's right hand was pressed to her temple. A little trickle of blood rolled down her cheek.

"I heard something and looked outside to see this poor woman on the sidewalk, groaning in pain." Randi clucked sympathetically.

"Where's Ronni?" Rex narrowed his eyes at his sister.

Of course he thought she did it. *I* thought she did it. It didn't take much to set his angry sister off. She'd already clocked me. And I was almost family. From the size of the wound, I'd say the weapon was a small squirrel or possibly a baby otter.

"You don't think Ronni hit her, do you?" Randi gasped but seemed unsure.

"Did you see anyone?" I asked Edna Lou.

The elderly woman shook her head. "No. I was just out for a walk, and something hit me. I heard someone running away, but that was it."

Rex drew his sister away to question her in private. I took her spot on the bench.

As much as I didn't want to, I had to ask, "Edna, were you here because of the house?"

She looked confused for a second. Then her eyes went wide, and she shook her head. "It probably looks that way, but no. We're only a few blocks from the cabin and a couple of blocks from my house. I really was just out for a stroll." She looked up at the house. "Wait…did you say Ronni Ferguson did it?"

"No," I said quickly. "The detective is just interviewing Ms. Ferguson."

Her eyes grew wide. "Ferguson? Like your fiancé?"

Crap.

I shrugged. "It's a small town. Yes, Randi and Ronni are Rex's twin sisters. But he's totally impartial." In fact, he'd probably arrest Ronni on the spot.

She shook her head sadly. "I didn't know. I am sorry to put you in this predicament with your donation."

"It's okay. You didn't know. Besides, Ronni doesn't like anyone. She hit me with a dead animal just the other day."

I regretted those words as soon as I said them. Would Edna Lou use those words against her in court?

"Did they take anything?" Rex joined us. "Money? Jewelry?"

Edna Lou checked her purse and wrist. "No." She reached into the pocket of her skirt, and a surprised look came over her as she pulled out a piece of paper.

*Stop nosing around for the treasure, or else.*

"This isn't mine!" She handed it to the detective and began to shiver, in spite of the heat.

I put my arm around her. "I'm sure it was just a prank."

She shook her head. "No, it isn't. I have been looking into the missing treasure. I've probably told half the town about it for the last few decades." She looked up at me sheepishly. "I'm a silly old woman. I thought maybe I had a claim…"

I finished her sentence for her. "…because you're a direct descendant of Peggy McMurtry."

Her eyes grew wide. "You knew?"

Either I could tell her I'd heard about it from the twins, or I could sound smart and say I figured it out. I went with smart.

"McMurtry…Murphy…your interest in the history of this town along with wanting this house to start a business…"

She sighed. "I should've told you. There's no reason to lie about it. I just didn't want you to think I was greedy."

I hugged her gingerly. "I wouldn't have thought that. And it's really none of my business."

When did I ever say that and mean it?

I toyed with telling her about my McMurtry ancestors, but I didn't know enough about it yet, and I didn't want to seem like I was interested in divvying up her claim.

"Ike and I always said we were going to buy this place and restore it. Open it up to the public. There's a lot of history there." She looked at the house.

"Edna," I said carefully, "remember what I told you Nels Larson said? That Ike said he was rich? Do you think he would've run off with the gold if he found it?"

If I were to describe the look on her face, I'd say she was horrified at the thought. "Ike wouldn't have done that! He was family! The only family I had left!"

"We did find that gold bar where his body had been in the cabin," I said.

After a moment of silence, she responded. "I believe he was bringing that to show me. To tell me the good news that he'd found the treasure. He wasn't going to run off. He was murdered for the gold."

"Well," I said, "that does align with what Nels said."

She threw up her hands. "Nels! That old fool thinks he knows everything! Ike didn't have a girlfriend and wasn't planning to skip town. I'm convinced of that."

Rex came over and waved me away. As I watched him interview Edna Lou from a distance, I realized I needed to visit the café the next morning. I had a couple of questions for Nels Larson.

After twenty minutes Rex joined me. "I'm sorry, Merry. Officer Dooley and I are going to have to canvass the area looking for witnesses. It might take all day."

I nodded. "Go ahead. And when you find the bastard who hit a little old lady, punch him in the throat for me."

Rex laughed, and I got in the car and drove home. Once at the house, I picked up the diary and looked at the other cover of the book. You couldn't be too thorough. Sure enough, there was the same small slit on the other side.

This time, there was only one page, and it wasn't a diary entry.

> *Tinkles, Tinkles little lamb*
> *How you wonder who I am.*
> *Meat and cheese and one red pear*
> *Rotting quietly on the stair*
> *Let's see that justice flies*
> *Spring the trap and watch him cry*
> *Then we will away to lunch*
> *With lots of hemp for you to munch.*

What did that mean?

I spent the rest of the day googling the poem, anagramming it out, and thinking. Was I wasting time on the rantings of a mad woman? Yes, I was.

By midevening, I got a text from Riley that said he was scoping out office space for his new private investigator practice. I texted back one word.

*Wubble.*

Let him google that and spend the next week wondering why I wanted a squid to impregnate his skull.

I needed to get out of this house and seek some advice. And I knew just who to turn to.

# CHAPTER EIGHTEEN

———

"She's *back*!" the scarlet macaw screeched as I entered the aviary. The other birds were sleeping…however birds sleep.

"Shut up," I said under my breath.

"*I heard that!*"

Mr. Fancy Pants was staring at me from behind the glass. I let myself in and sat down next to him with a baggie full of crumbled shortbread cookies. He attacked them like a demon possessed.

"Are they not feeding you?" I asked.

He didn't answer.

"She's talking to that damn bird again!" the macaw complained.

Just how much did that kid talk about me? Clearly, he repeated phrases so often that the parrot picked them up. I'd report him, but they might find out about my nighttime visits to my vulture.

"What am I going to do when they send you back?" I asked.

The raptor looked up at me as if he hadn't thought about it. I'd be willing to bet that the National Zoo didn't include Girl Scout Cookies as part of a healthy diet. Would they allow me to adopt him permanently? I could send him care packages.

While he ate, I filled him in on the nuanced details of the murders past and present. I'd like to think he cared. But deep down I knew this was just a bizarre form of therapy for me. And way cheaper than Susan. One thing about Fancy Pants—he did seem a tad more judgmental than my human therapist. In a weird way, I liked that.

The cookies were gone, and the bird stuck his head in my purse. When he didn't find any cookies, he began pacing. Scientists suspect these raptors have a keen sense of smell. I didn't have any more treats on me, but maybe he didn't fully trust me.

"She's gonna make him *fat*!" the parrot screeched. "Then they'll blame *me*!"

The other birds were awake and getting agitated, so it was time to take my leave. I thanked the vulture, who watched me head for the door.

A shadow passed at the other end of the building, and I dropped to the floor. Was the kid here? Did he know that the macaw talked about him? I low-crawled to the door to Fancy Pants' enclosure and slipped through, closing it behind me, when I heard a door at the other end of the room slam.

I was out of the building before anyone could discover my illegal feeding of a protected animal. I wanted Mr. Fancy Pants to stay at Obladi Zoo as long as possible.

Once outside, I was about to head for the closest gate when I heard footsteps coming from that direction. What was going on here? Were all the staff here for one night? I'd better find another way.

I paused to hide behind the camel and llama enclosure. A large llama was munching on some straw. No, wait. He was chewing on the twine around the straw. Wow. Twine. Too bad the girls didn't check the zoo during the scavenger hunt.

As usual, I was distracted by something ridiculous—it was so hard to focus these days. Maybe I was losing my mind. I had to keep moving. The sound of people whispering was coming my way.

The statue for Tinkles stared at me as I made my way around it. A noise came from behind me, and I tripped and fell. As I dropped, my keys, carefully laced through my fingers, cut deep into the statue as I flailed to stop my fall.

Great. I just keyed a llama. I shoved my keys into my pocket and ran...headfirst into what felt like a sledgehammer. The last thing I remember as I hit the concrete was the looming, statue of Tinkles looking down on me.

I came to in complete darkness. The back of my head hurt where I'd been punched. Had they hit me and run? I sat up and didn't see the statue. I put my hand on the ground, but it wasn't concrete. It was dirt and straw. Where was I?

Definitely outside. Clouds obscured any light. Whoever had clobbered me had moved me, but to where?

There was an earthy smell. When you live in Iowa long enough, you get used to the smell of animals and manure. Those smells surrounded me now. Well, it was a zoo...

Getting to my feet was a bit harder than usual as my skull throbbed and I felt lightheaded. Well, wherever I was, I was leaving. Who hit me? Could it be that the kid in the aviary had had enough of me once and for all? Seemed a bit extreme.

There was a sound off to my right in the darkness. A low, guttural sound. Not quite a growl. Blood turned to ice in my veins. Was I in an enclosure? With wild animals? Now I was starting to regret my nocturnal visit to the king vulture.

I didn't hear voices anymore. Whoever had dumped me here was gone. I looked around in the dim light to get my bearings. I was definitely behind bars. On the other side, directly in front of me was the carousel. Off to my right I recognized the shadow of the train tracks. I closed my eyes and pictured the map.

The aviary was on my left, so I wasn't too far away from where I'd started. The reptile house would be on my right, which meant I was near the cages where the snow leopard, jaguar, and lions were.

*Roooooooooar!*

Scratch that. I was *in* the cages where the big cats were. And all I had on me was an empty box of Girl Scout Cookies.

Oh man.

# CHAPTER NINTEEN

———

They say that your entire life flashes before your eyes when you're about to die. That was true. It had happened to me in Eastern Europe when I'd been chased by a chicken with an Uzi, and in Argentina when I'd been attacked by a herd of rabid capybaras.

It certainly was going through my head as I heard the pacing of a giant cat nearby. I shoved those thoughts aside as unhelpful. Another roar came from my left. Two cats. And from the sound, I guessed that these were the two female lions they had here.

Which meant the male was also nearby, but I didn't need to worry about him. The biggest threat came from the females who hunted me now. Not much of a relief. What did I know about lions? Well, they were big and had lots of teeth and claws.

I stayed still for the moment. If I ran, they'd run, and even though I look like I'm in good shape…I'm not. I was also regretting a lifetime of Oreo binging right about now. And ravioli. But to these ladies, I just smelled like yummy, yummy meat.

Whoever had dumped me in here had left me to die. On the good side, it meant I was getting too close to solving the case. On the bad side, the good side wasn't much consolation.

*Think, Merry!* What could I use? I had keys in my pocket I could interlace through my fingers as a sort of weapon again. But that would just make these kitties angry. Kitties! These were just big domestic cats. Well, ginormous domestic cats. Cats that outweighed me by a *lot*.

The clouds vanished, and a bright, full moon illuminated the enclosure. You might think that was a plus because I could see my surroundings, and you'd be right if it weren't for the fact that I could now see two giant predators, one on either side of me, planning how their new surprise snack was going to go down.

Ten feet in front of me was the fence. I'd scaled one just like it many times before. But it was built for that, because these cats could climb. Near the top, the fence leaned inward. I could probably pull myself over that. But would I be fast enough?

Four feet off to my right, between me and one of the lions, was an eight-foot-tall fake tree with long branches. I could climb that faster than the fence, but it had the unfortunate issue of being the premium chaise lounges for the beasts at their own Club Med. Which meant I'd only hold the advantage for a few seconds before the Merry munching began.

I needed a zookeeper…a safari leader. Hell, I'd take a taxidermist about now. I was pretty sure Ronni could take them, but the way she felt about me right now—she'd probably hose me down with bacon grease.

The cats were pacing faster now, their mouths open in anticipation of my deliciousness. They say you are what you eat. Would I taste like junk food to them? That probably wasn't the most helpful thought to have at this moment.

Should I call for help? Whoever threw me in here hadn't stuck around to see what happened. Which was weird because I would have. No…I was pretty sure I was on my own here.

"Whoa," I said softly. "Big kitties! Nice kitties!"

What was I doing? That didn't work on Philby and Martini! Why did I think it would work on these two? If only I had a tin of tuna…

It was down to a run for the fence or a short respite from certain death in the tree. What a decision. And I was running out of time to make it.

The first lion made it for me. She reached out and swatted in my direction. I broke and ran like hell for the fence. I jumped, my fingers gripping the bars as I used my feet and hands to climb as fast as I could.

Two loud roars came from below, and I felt a huge paw hit the back of my leg. I pulled myself a little higher, but my sweaty hands were making me slip.

The first lion jumped at me. One of its claws hooked into my tennis shoe. I kicked away, and the animal dropped with the shoe in its mouth. There was no time to celebrate, as the other female launched herself into the air. I barely had time to bring my legs up, and she barely missed me.

My muscles were screaming, and my fingers were slipping. This was it. I was a goner. I hoped that Rex would take care of my cats, that Riley would give a *professional* eulogy at my funeral, and that Randi and Ronni wouldn't try to stuff me.

There was a strange cry above. I reached up and managed to grab hold of the bars, but the cats were throwing their whole weight against the bars now, and the vibrations were working against me by weakening my grip.

"*Why don't girls like me?*" The macaw, followed closely by Mr. Fancy Pants, swept into the enclosure and dove at the lions, who dropped to the ground in confusion.

That was all I needed. It took everything I had to scale the fence up to the point where the bars went inward. It took only a few seconds to get over that hurdle and drop down the other side.

The macaw and the king vulture flew up out of the pen, to my relief, and dove back into the aviary. I guess I hadn't fully closed the door to Mr. Fancy Pants' little room.

"*Stupid Girl Scout Cookies!*" I heard the parrot shriek in the distance.

Inside the enclosure, one of the lions had retreated into the darkness while the other gnawed on my shoe. I made it into the nearest bathroom to check my leg. It wasn't as bad as I'd thought. I tore off part of my T-shirt to make a tourniquet and left it at that.

And then I limped off to my car and drove to Kelly's house.

"Why did you come here?" Kelly asked as she cleaned my wounds.

"Ouch!" I flinched. "Because I don't want Rex to know what happened."

Finn and Robert were asleep, which was good because the fewer people who knew about this, the better.

Kelly pulled out a round needle and started to thread it. "You'll need stitches. If you don't want Rex to see these, you'll have to wear pants for a while."

I lay down on my stomach and clenched my teeth until she was done. She covered the leg with a large piece of gauze and taped it. Then she slapped me on my butt and handed me a bottle of aspirin.

"What?" I stared at the generic bottle. "Not the good stuff?"

Kelly glared at me. "Anyone who breaks into a zoo to talk to a vulture and ends up in the lion pen doesn't deserve the good stuff."

She followed me home, and I limped inside. In the bedroom, when I saw my reflection, I realized that if Rex had seen me, he'd probably call the wedding off. My T-shirt was torn to the midriff. There was straw in my hair, and there was an impressive paw print on my other shoe.

I stripped and took a shower, careful to hang my torn leg out of the tub. Philby hissed at my destroyed clothing. And as I climbed into a pair of pajama pants and a nightshirt, I decided she could've taken one of the beasts. Kelly made sure I was in bed before leaving me to my fate.

As I lay in bed, I realized that if the macaw and Mr. Fancy Pants hadn't come to my rescue, I'd be nothing but a side of beef right now. Ignoring Kelly's instructions, I took a handful of Tylenol PM and passed out.

\* \* \*

My cell buzzed like it was on fire. My eyes still closed, I answered it.

Kelly spoke. "You made the news. Zoo officials are looking to find out who the lions ate last night. They found your shoe. They're calling it a suicide."

"Well, that's nice. Rex will probably think I had something to do with it."

She agreed. "The police are investigating, but they don't have much to go on other than the remains of a white sneaker."

"Sounds like an unsolved case to me," I mumbled.

My eyelids were so heavy, and my whole body hurt. My bruises had bruises.

"Should I come over and take a look at you?"

"Are you going to put me out of my misery?" I asked, only half joking.

"No. You enjoy being in misery too much. Get some sleep. I'll stop by after my shift."

We hung up, and I took four aspirin pills. I had to get up. I had an old men's coffee klatch to invade.

\* \* \*

The café in town was literally named The Café. Not very original, I know, but it did make it easy to describe to new people when they wanted to know where to get coffee and fairly decent home cooking.

It was also the site of a daily meeting of all of the old men in town. In high school I'd worked there as a waitress. And while some of those old men weren't with us anymore, you could be sure the ranks were still full. Monday through Friday morning from six a.m. until nine, you could find twenty to twenty-five men sitting around, drinking coffee, and complaining about the weather—for which in Iowa, there was a lot of material.

The minute I walked in, Nels, dressed in an unseasonably warm long-sleeved T-shirt and khaki pants, spotted me. With these guys, ninety degrees was considered just above freezing. They didn't even notice that I was overdressed for the weather.

I walked over, and Nels motioned to a chair next to him. Without hesitation, I sat, becoming the youngest person at the table by at least thirty years.

"What are you doing here, little lady?" Nels grinned and waved a waitress over.

I ordered a hot tea. "I just was passing by and saw you here. It reminded me I had a question for you."

"Gentlemen!" Nels tapped his spoon on his coffee mug. "This is Merry. I met her the other day. Merry, this is everyone."

Half of the men were wearing muddy overalls, and all of them mumbled a hello before going back to their conversations.

"So what did you want to ask me?"

My tea arrived, and I squeezed the rest of the bag into it before taking a sip. "I have a friend who's looking to move here. I wondered if they'd put Ike's house on the market yet?"

I couldn't just go in, both barrels blazing with direct questions, now could I? These old guys were wary. They thought giving their social security number to the bank would lead to hackers stealing their pickup trucks.

Nels smiled. "Is she pretty?"

"Oh yes. Gorgeous." You couldn't be offended by questions like that. And I was pretty sure my imaginary friend could handle the likes of wizened old Nels Larson.

"I haven't seen a sign up yet," he said. "Some of these real estate agents are vultures, always swooping in at the wrong moment. Why, Fred over there..." He pointed to a man who looked like Gollum. Gollum waved back. "Two days after his sister died, a real estate agent showed up at the funeral and gave him her card. Can you believe that?"

"No," I said.

"Now, Ike's funeral has taken a little time. I imagine Edna Lou is handling things. Anyway, I'll just bet one of them vultures shows up at the funeral to try to sell the house."

I hadn't thought about Ike's funeral. Huh. The murder happened a few days ago, so maybe the autopsy put things off. But I was sure Edna Lou would be handling the arrangements.

"Maybe Ike's girlfriend wants it?" I asked with a big smile.

He shook his head. "I haven't seen that woman in a couple of days. I didn't like her. Always parking in my driveway instead of Ike's."

"Did you talk to her?" I pressed.

"Not really. She just scowled at me before going into the house. She had keys, you see."

That was one question answered.

"I talked to Edna Lou, and she said Ike didn't have a girlfriend."

"I was surprised too! Ike didn't really seem that way, if you catch my drift."

I did. After seeing the wigs and ladies' clothing at the other house, I really did.

"Did Ike have any hobbies?" I still wanted to find out about the animal skeletons.

Nels rubbed his chin. "Wanted to get into taxidermy, he said. I only ever saw a couple of skeletons he had. I explained that taxidermy meant preserving the animals in a way that makes them look like they were still alive. And then those taxidermy ladies moved into the Peters place. He kind of lost interest then."

"Randi and Ronni Ferguson?" I asked innocently. "I know them."

Nels broke into a huge smile. "Would you introduce me? I kind of like the angry one."

I promised to do just that as I finished my tea and tossed a five on the table. Nels thanked me for coming, and I fled to the outside.

Well, at least I get the flamingo and penguin skeletons. And Nels kind of confirmed the wig and the women's clothes too. But he wasn't very helpful about Penelope May. Not that he could do anything about that.

Penelope was definitely my number one suspect. I wondered if she was the one who tried to kill me at the zoo. And why was she there, late at night? I took out my keys, and something glinted in the sun.

My keys were covered in some sort of gold-like dust. That was strange. How did that get there? I only recalled using them at the…

I dialed Rex as I raced to my car, demanding he meet me at the zoo. Because I was closer and knew some sweet trick racing skills, I was there before him, with my paid ticket, standing in front of the Tinkles statue.

There were three long grooves down the side from where I'd keyed the statue on my way to the ground. Kneeling on the cement, I looked closer. I ran my fingers through the ruts. And came away with gold dust.

"I got a call from the zoo that someone was doing unmentionable things to the llama statue," Rex's voice said from behind me.

"I think I've found the bulk of Mad Mimi's gold." I showed him my fingers.

Rex got down on the ground and read the plaque that said the statue was donated by his sisters. Before I could say anything else, he called them. Seconds later, after asking one question, he turned to me.

"They found the statue in the basement and donated it to the zoo. This llama was in the Peters' house for as long as anyone could remember. And it was too heavy to move…"

"…because it's made out of solid gold," I finished.

A couple of officers arrived and cordoned off the area while Rex talked to the zoo director. I couldn't take my eyes off the statue. Here was Mimi's fortune, hiding in plain sight. Somehow she'd had it sculpted and added layer of cement or something like that, coating it.

And no one ever knew the truth.

Rex joined me. "Of course, the zoo wants to claim the treasure. Randi and Ronni will also likely submit a claim."

I thought about Edna Lou. She'd waited her whole life to see this. After getting quick permission from Rex, I called her. She arrived within a few minutes and stood in front of the llama, entranced.

By then Rex had chipped off a chunk of plaster the size of an orange. Gold glittered in the sunlight. This was the real thing. And all these years it had been sitting in the Ferguson basement.

So why were there gold bars out there? Did they have too much gold for the statue? And did Ike know about this?

"I can't believe it," Edna said softly. "All these years it was in the basement of that house. And then it was donated here. How? Why?"

An idea swirled around in my head. I explained the hidden pages in Mehitable's diary. "Eustace kept the gold for her when she was worried about her cousin, Peggy. Maybe when Mehitable died, he had this made in Tinkles' memory?"

She shook her head. "But, why not use it? Or donate the gold? Why do this?"

I shrugged. "We keep hearing that he didn't need the money. Maybe he just wanted to honor her. Maybe he thought this was funny. A gag. We'll never know, but that's my theory."

Rex joined us. "I've got a crew coming right now to take it down and deliver it to my station for tests."

If it occurred to Edna Lou that as a descendant she might have a claim to it, she didn't say so. It had to be a shock. The three of us watched as the statue was dug up and carried to a truck.

"I guess that is one mystery solved." Edna touched the bruise at her temple. "Detective, would it be alright if I went home? I'm not feeling very well."

Rex and I walked her to her car, watching to see if she was dizzy. She insisted she could manage and drove away.

"I guess that's over," I said as I watched her.

Rex gave me a look. "Merry, how did you know about the statue?"

Uh-oh. In my zeal to find the truth, I'd neglected to come up with a reason why I knew about the statue.

My silence seemed to be all he needed.

"It was you in the lion pen, wasn't it?" His voice was calm as he ran his hands through his hair. Normally, I found this action endearing, but this time I felt bad. I was the cause of his frustration. That didn't feel very good.

"Um…yes?" I smiled weakly. "But it isn't what you think."

"You broke into the zoo and ended up in the lion pen. Honestly, I'm not sure what I think." Instead of anger, his eyes were full of fear.

My actions had frightened him. I had to admit, they frightened me too.

"Does it help to tell you I went to visit Mr. Fancy Pants and was clocked by someone who dumped me in the lion pen?"

A vein I'd never noticed before throbbed on Rex's forehead. That wasn't good.

"You were assaulted?" His voice wavered with emotion. "And you didn't tell me? Are you okay?"

"I've been in worse situations when I was with the CIA," I said.

"But you're not with the CIA. You're retired," he replied. "Merry! You could've been killed."

"That's true, but this isn't my fault. Well, not totally." To be fair, I shouldn't have broken into the zoo in the first place. Rex was probably going to tell the staff, and I'd be banned.

"We thought someone had died," he continued. "We were looking through missing person reports."

My jaw dropped. "We have missing persons in Who's There? Who?"

Rex closed his eyes and pinched the bridge of his nose. I'd never seen him do that. The detective had been replaced by my fiancé. A concerned and worried fiancé.

"Alright, I was wrong to go to the zoo and wrong not to report the assault."

"The law," my fiancé said very, very slowly, "applies to everyone. It applies to you. But you act like it doesn't." He threw his hands up into the air. "I have no idea what to do with this information. Filing a report just gets you deeper into trouble. And I'll probably get into trouble."

I hadn't thought of that. My actions impacted Rex's job. This wouldn't be a good time to mention my breaking in to both of Ike's houses.

"And I think you broke into Ike's house," he finished.

He had me there.

I sighed heavily. "Okay. I broke into the house near me. And that's how I knew Penelope May had the gold bars. I witnessed her taking them."

We stood there for a very long time.

"Go home," Rex finally said. "I can't think about this today. I just can't." He walked away.

What had I done?

My cell rang, and I answered.

"Merry! Can you come by the house? I have something for you!" Randi hung up before I could turn her down.

It seemed like the perfect distraction. I was there in minutes, and she met me at the door.

"Come in! I have the perfect thing for the wedding!"

I didn't want to tell her I was pretty sure there wouldn't be a wedding due to my illegal extracurricular activities. She seemed so happy. I followed her into the former dining room.

"Stay here! I'll be right back!" And with that, Randi vanished.

Ronni appeared in her place, arms folded over her chest. "I can't believe my brother is marrying *you*! But then, he's an idiot."

I didn't ignore her. Not this time. "Your brother is an amazing man! He's not an idiot...I am!"

Wait. Did I mean to say that?

Ronni smiled for the first time since I'd met her. She almost laughed, which terrified me because I was pretty sure that the laughter from someone so hateful would cause angels to explode. As she walked away, I breathed a sigh of relief.

In the corner, I spotted the stepladder. At least I could check something out. I set it up underneath the ceiling where those little holes were.

My cell phone had a ruler app. It was pretty cool and had been a lifesaver several times, from measuring arts and crafts projects to the impressive skid of cat barf (Philby holds the record at a foot and a half). It's proven useful.

I held my phone up to the one hole farthest away. Three feet from the wall. Two feet in were the two little holes, side by side. They were a foot from the wall. An idea started forming, and I scooted the stepladder closer to the wall by scooting it from the top step. I do not recommend doing this.

About a foot down from the ceiling was a rusty nail. How long had that been there?

"What are you doing up there?" Randi asked as she walked in with a remote control.

"Just checking something. Randi"—I climbed down— "how long has this nail been here?"

She squinted. "Oh, that? I was told it's original to the house. Something about the kind of plaster it's stuck in—taking it out would result in a huge hole. I guess no one has thought of doing that."

"It's been here since the original owners?"

She shrugged. "That's what the real estate agent said. Now come down from there. I want to show you something."

As I stood on the ground before her, all kinds of thoughts were swirling through my head.

"I got the idea from Mad Mimi!" Randi pressed a button, and a huge llama rolled into the room.

A huge dead llama with wheels attached to its hooves. It wore some sort of blanket that said *Congratulations, Rex and Merry!*

I decided it was time to embrace the weird. "I love it! Can I try?"

Randi beamed as she handed me the remote. "Isn't it great? We'd had this llama for weeks. It's from the zoo in Omaha. When you guys were talking about Mehitable's llama, Tinkles, I knew it was perfect!"

The controls were impressive. The body didn't wobble on its skinny legs. I steered it around the room. It was kind of like those remote-controlled cars.

"This is pretty amazing," I said, just as I steered it into a wall. "Whoa…"

A lightbulb went off in my head. I had an idea. I asked Randi if I could set up a little experiment. She agreed.

I got to work.

# CHAPTER TWENTY

———

It took most of the day to pull together the resources I needed. Sadly, Rex didn't call or text or even ask what I was up to. Randi and Ronni left me alone for a couple of hours as they had to go check out a dead two-headed goat at a farm. This was considered to be the holy grail for taxidermists, and they left, muttering something about making a mythological hydra.

When I finally got home, I made a number of phone calls to Rex (who let it go to voicemail), Edna Lou (who didn't know what voicemail was), and Kelly. Everything was set for nine in the morning the next day.

In spite of the excitement I felt about my discovery, I couldn't help feel like a complete fool. For two years I'd ignored every warning Rex had given me about getting involved in police matters.

He had to be mad. The trouble was that he was frustrated with me. Multiple times during our relationship, he'd asked me to stop messing around. I'd almost been killed a number of times—which to me registered as another day in the office.

But to my fiancé, I was being disrespectful. Thumbing my nose at his job and making him think I didn't care what he said. What was wrong with me?

I was pretty sure he'd be impressed in the morning when I revealed my news. But it wouldn't do anything to patch this mess up. As I went to bed that night, I had no idea what would fix things.

"What are we doing here?" Rex asked. There wasn't any malice—more like *let's humor my crazy ex-fiancé.*

My heart crashed into my shoes. Rex would never yell at me or get into an argument in public. But I still knew I'd gone too far this time.

"I know who killed Mehitable," I said as brightly as I could, considering I felt like my shoe in the lion's jaws.

Edna was wandering through the house, fascinated or horrified (you'd be surprised how often those emotions are confused) by the many dead beasts acting out human scenes. Inviting her to this little reveal was about as dicey as inviting Rex.

"Well?" He folded his arms over his chest.

"I'm waiting for someone else."

Just then the door opened and ten little girls poured in, accompanied by Kelly and Dr. Soo Jin Body.

"You invited your troop?" Rex's mouth hung open.

"Yes. They couldn't be there when we found the treasure. I thought they'd like this." I waved the girls in, but with what they were seeing around them, they weren't moving fast.

"Wow!" Inez reached out and touched a skunk in a lab coat.

"This is the coolest place ever!" one of the Kaitlyns said. And the rest agreed.

For ten minutes the girls squealed over every single taxidermized animal. I couldn't blame them.

Randi led them on a tour, and the girls loved her immediately. Ronni stood in the kitchen door, a scowl etched into her face.

"Stop touching things!" she screamed more than once.

Betty, ever fearless, walked right up to her. "What do you do with their guts? And their eyeballs?"

Ronni stared at the child who was almost her size. I was ready in case she tried to hit her with a duck.

After a beat she said, "Want to see?"

Betty promptly exploded with glee. I almost exploded with shock. Ronni liked someone? A human? Or was she just luring the little girl into a trap and I'd have one less child in my troop?

"The Hannahs couldn't come," Kelly said as she joined me. "They're on a trip with their families to Iowa City."

At last everyone crowded into the dining room. No one looked at the ceiling, which meant they weren't expecting what was coming. That was fun. I asked Kelly to be Mehitable, and the girls let out a loud scream of approval.

My best friend took her place. And I brought in the remote-controlled llama. The squeal for that was even louder. Rex gently shook his head. I wasn't sure if that meant he didn't like the llama or we weren't getting married.

I swallowed the lump that formed in my throat.

It took a couple of attempts to get the llama into position. I stood by the wall with the little nail in it, next to the llama.

"I know who killed Mehitable Peters," I said dramatically, indicating Kelly.

I had their rapt attention now.

I reached up and cut a thin rope that was tied to the nail. The rope ran through a loop in the ceiling, underneath the axe handle where it connected to the axe-head, through another loop on the other side, then back to another loop above the butt of the handle, through the hole in the handle, and back to a knot in the second loop. As the rope released the front of the handle, the rubber axe came swinging down, clocking Kelly in the forehead. The last of the rope released from the final loop, and the whole axe came down.

"Mehitable had rigged the rope because someone was stealing food."

The faces around me looked confused, but I didn't have time to explain.

Pointing at the nail, I continued, "She tied the rope that went through the two loops, underneath the axe-head. Well, the neck really. The axe swung down, and the rope through the hole in the end of the axe fell away, making the whole axe fall to the floor."

Dr. Soo Jin's eyes grew wide, I think with excitement. I'd like to think it was with excitement. "She accidentally killed herself?"

I shook my head. "Nope. Tinkles chewed through the rope. And I'm guessing he ate the rest of the rope after the accident."

"The llama did it?" Edna shrieked.

I nodded. "In her diary Mehitable talks about Tinkles eating stuff inside the house, furniture, et cetera. She also says she did something to catch the thief. We know she had a camera rigged up to take a picture. There was the outline of something in a reflection in the picture. I'd be willing to bet when it comes back from the state police, we will see a picture of Tinkles."

I pointed at the nail and the llama. He (or she—I didn't think it polite to ask) was just the right height.

"She wasn't murdered?" Edna squeaked.

I immediately felt sorry for her. She'd been hoping for a juicy murder. Not death by an unwitting (unless the giant purple cat was behind it) pet.

"It's still a very interesting story. The llama that killed its owner," I said eagerly.

Edna kind of half nodded.

"I love it!" Soo Jin said.

Lauren spoke up. "Whoa. That's bad for Mad Mimi, but it's cool how she rigged that up."

I had to agree. We all turned to look at Rex.

He studied the apparatus, and Kelly lay down on the floor like she was dead. An action the girls appreciated.

"I think you're right, Wrath" was all he said.

While everyone celebrated and Caterina and Emily played with the remote-controlled llama, I was upset. Oh sure, I should be happy that I'd solved that case. But there was just one problem. Rex called me "Wrath." He only did that in professional situations.

Was I no longer "Merry"?

"That's crazy." Kelly stood next to me. "How did you figure it out?"

"It was the llama at the zoo eating twine, and the holes in the ceiling. They are just the right length to hold up an axe." I was talking to her but looking at Rex, who was engaged in conversation with the girls.

"Why's Rex mad at you?" Kelly followed my gaze.

"He found out it was me in the lion's pen." I told her the whole story, about the gold on my keys and the treasure inside the statue.

"The llama statue at Obladi Zoo was made of gold?" she cried.

All eyes turned to us to stare.

"That heavy thing from the basement?" Ronni scowled. "That's been there for years. The real estate agent told us it was too heavy to move, so none of the previous owners did. We got it out of here because we need the space"—she winked at Betty— "for the guts and eyeballs."

As stunned as I was to see Ronni wink, I picked it up. "Eustace had the gold. My guess is he figured out that Tinkles chewed through the rope and killed his sister. He didn't need it, or maybe didn't want it after this, so I think he had the statue made."

"But why?" Randi raised her hand, which was adorable. "Why not just spend it?"

I shrugged. "I think it was a tribute to his sister."

Edna piped up. "But what about the maps?"

"That, I'm not sure of," I answered. "Maybe he made them for fun for his kids? The map was on his farm. It could've been something entirely different. A game."

"I think that's a good explanation," Rex said, staring at me with a meaning I didn't get.

Maybe things weren't so bad after all. One murder down…one to go.

# CHAPTER TWENTY-ONE

In spite of my amazing super sleuth skills, Rex avoided me. I spent the rest of the day, coasting on my laurels, and the next depressed because it was possible I'd blown my relationship with the man I was supposed to marry.

How did this go so wrong? Oh. Right. I was an idiot. A woman who couldn't give up the thrill of the chase. Susan had pointed out to me a short while ago that my career had ended abruptly and too early. I'd gone from exotic galas in Warsaw and deadly shootouts in Austria to Girl Scout camp in Who's There.

Not that I was complaining. I loved my troop. They restored my sense of fun and possibly encouraged me in my secret exploits. But being chased through the streets of Rio by a Bolivian hit man was more exciting than learning how to make a bowline hitch knot.

I was flunking adulthood.

To be fair, things just sort of happened to me. As far as dead bodies went. The fact that I didn't leave things to the professionals was where I needed some work. And now my fiancé, the detective whose cases these were, knew I wouldn't give up.

Was I an adrenaline junkie? If so, it made sense that the only adrenaline I'd found in my small hometown was related to dangerous murderers. That wasn't normal. Why couldn't I be like Kelly or Soo Jin (maybe especially Soo Jin)?

At this point, with my wedding five months away, the dress ordered and things falling into place, I needed to analyze my feelings.

Did I love Rex? Yes. Enough to spend the rest of my life with him? Yes. Enough to move in with him and sell my house?

I couldn't answer that. Seemed to me if I couldn't answer that simple question, I wasn't ready to get married. Then again, Rex and I had dated two years before he popped the question. That seemed like a reasonable length of time to figure out what I wanted.

Did I want to marry Rex?

Philby had been staring at me for hours. I was pretty sure she hadn't blinked once during that whole time.

"What do you think?" I asked her.

She lifted her considerable bulk and walked over to me. Martini was asleep, on her back, folded over the armrest of the couch.

"Well?" I pressed the feline führer. "I *know* you have an opinion."

Philby sat down next to me and threw up on my lap. The noise startled Martini awake, but it didn't last. Then, my cat farted and walked away.

My Hitler cat thought I was an idiot too.

I went to my bedroom and changed my clothes, returning to find the very last person I wanted to see today.

Riley.

"Why are you in my house?"

He smiled and patted the seat on the couch next to him. I took a seat in the chair opposite.

"I just wanted to tell you that I've decided to retire. And I've rented office space. It'll take a few months to get my license. And then I'll open up shop."

My jaw dropped. "You were serious?" Riley was rarely serious about anything, and that included the time when he was "dating" a receptionist at the Ukrainian Embassy who tried to kill him with a sharpened curling iron.

Riley smiled and leaned back on the couch. He even managed to avoid the wet spot where Philby had barfed.

"I'm tired of all this government crap. There's a lot going on around here. You're solving one-hundred-year-old murders and dodging lions. Even life as a Fed isn't that interesting."

I folded my arms over my chest. "How did you know about the lions?"

He had the nerve to wink. "That is one perk of being in the FBI—we have access to surveillance that most police don't even have. Satellites."

My eyes nearly popped out of my head—which wouldn't have been a good look for me.

"You saw what happened?"

He nodded.

"Can I get a copy of that?" I asked.

Riley laughed out loud. "You really aren't ready for a domestic life, are you?"

My eyes narrowed. "It just so happens you're wrong. Because I *don't know* what I'm ready for."

He held up his hands defensively. "Alright, alright. Don't get mad. I'm just here because I have a proposition for you."

That was all I needed. A proposition from an ex-boyfriend just as I was trying to save my relationship with Rex.

"It's not what you think." He wiggled his eyebrows suggestively. "It's a job. I was wondering if you'd want to work for me."

I stared at him. I didn't see that coming.

"I don't want to interfere with your life. But I know the local police and sheriff's department have warned you off their cases. As an investigator, you'd be legitimate."

"Legitimately crazy, you mean," I said.

He got up and handed me a business card. "Think about it. It'll be about three months before I'm ready."

I scowled. "I thought it took a year to get certified." Not that I'd looked into that…or anything.

"Six months minimum usually." He grinned. "I have a friend who is moving my application with the private investigator licensing services bureau. She said with my experience with the CIA and FBI, it's a no-brainer."

"Already schmoozing pretty girls to get what you want?"

Riley smiled as he walked to the door. "Just think about it. I'll be in touch."

As he left, I turned the card over.

Son of a bimbo! He wasn't opening up an office in Des Moines! This address was for Main Street Who's There!

Whether I wanted the job or not, I was going to kill him.

This was followed by a polite knock on the door. Rex stood there holding out a large envelope and a long box.

"I thought you'd want to return these to Edna Lou," he said casually. "You were right. The analysis of the photo showed a distinct llama shape in the reflection. And there was rope in the handle's hole."

"Do you want to come in for a cup of coffee?" Why did I say that? I didn't have coffee. And Rex knew it.

He shook his head. "I should get back. By the way—was that Riley Andrews I saw driving off?"

"Yeah," I said. "He just dropped by to say he's retiring from the FBI." There was no way I was telling Rex about Riley's scheme or job offer.

He ran his hand through his hair. "Look, Merry, I'm not trying to avoid you. I just need some time to process things."

I swallowed hard. "Of course. I understand."

He said goodbye, and as I closed the door, I felt terrible. What was I going to do if he decided to break off the wedding?

No! I wasn't going to think about that. I scooped up my keys, the axe, and the envelope. At least taking these things to Edna would cheer me up.

The cabin door was open when I got to the park. Angry voices argued inside. I walked in, and to my complete surprise, saw Penelope May and Edna Lou squaring off. The younger woman was larger than the elderly historian and outweighed her by at least fifty pounds. Fists were clenched. Faces were red.

"What are you doing here?" I demanded.

Penelope May must be trying to shake down Edna Lou to see if she knew where the rest of the gold was.

"Stay out of this," the woman growled.

Her eyes froze on me in what looked like recognition. I hoped she didn't remember me from Ike's house.

"You leave this woman alone!" I stepped between her and Edna Lou. "I know you killed Ike and made off with a few of his gold bars!"

This made the woman freeze. It was as if I was accusing her of stealing from widows and orphans. The look of incredulity on her face brought me up short.

"Edna?" I turned to look at the older woman. "Are you okay? Did she hurt you?"

Edna looked past me with an expression of alarm just before my head exploded with pain and everything went black.

\* \* \*

"…a terrible idea," a muffled voice said through a gauzy veil of pain. It might have been something else like *a terrible hyena* or something about IKEA. The voices were far off, and my head felt like it had been run over by a truck.

It was dark, and I was tied, ankles to wrists, on a floor. A sliver of light at the far wall told me I was in a room and someone was just outside the door.

At least I wasn't in with lions again…wait… I sniffed the air and listened closely. It didn't seem like I was in with the big cats. The worst would be to be in a room with monkeys. I didn't like monkeys.

Oh sure, you're wondering why, since I'm obviously enamored with animals. Not monkeys. Of any type. I even avoided the monkey house at the zoo.

It wasn't that I was afraid of them. I wasn't saying I wasn't afraid of anything, because I was afraid of a lot, really. Things like asphyxiation, something happening to my cats, Betty armed with a flamethrower…the usual stuff.

I just didn't like monkeys, especially chimpanzees. Chimps will hunt, kill, and eat their own. They are notoriously dangerous and have no problem flinging crap in your general direction. And don't get me started about pictures of chimps in business suits. *Shudder.*

Owwww! My head throbbed just to think about it. I remembered getting clocked by Penelope May. Did she hurt Edna Lou? Because if she did, I was going to kill her.

That would really mess things up with Rex. He wouldn't like it if I was a murderous felon. He'd definitely call the wedding off for that.

I hated being hog-tied with my ankles and wrists behind me. First of all, it hurts. Secondly, I wasn't that flexible, and third, it was really hard to escape from. Lying on my side, my shoulders and quads burning, I tried to touch the ropes that held me. Yup. Good, strong knots. Probably a bowline. You know, in my few years as a scout leader, I never could master that one. The only girls in my troop who did were Lauren and Betty.

Did Lauren and Betty kidnap me? Whoa. I really was brained if I thought that. My girls loved me. Well, they put up with me.

I strained at my bonds and was rewarded with searing pain. Any movement tugged on my extremities in a very unpleasant way. Penelope was strong. I wondered where she'd learned to hog-tie a person like that. Maybe she was a rodeo clown. I always thought rodeo clowns were shifty. Like they were just biding their time.

"Where's the gold?" Penelope's voice came through loud and clear.

Oh no! Was she torturing Edna Lou? I hoped not. It wasn't dangerous intel. The police had the llama statue. There was no way Penelope was getting that. Unless she was going for a trade.

And being engaged to the one police detective in town made me an excellent victim. Would Rex trade the gold llama for me? Sadly, I was sure that ship had sailed. As I slid into a self-pity fest that would impress a tween drama queen, I was fearful for Edna.

That woman was so frail, hitting her even lightly might kill her. And there were so many things the two of us hadn't done yet—like find out if we were related, tracing our family tree, picking wildflowers in a meadow in springtime…

My concussion was making me delirious. Or concussions. I'd had a lot of those lately. Maybe I should start wearing a bicycle helmet.

I shook it off, causing another surge of pain in my joints. I really had to stop doing that. It was time to think. I needed an escape plan.

"Noooooooooo!" Edna Lou wailed from the other room.

I was running out of time.

Okay, there had to be something else in this room—something I could use to cut through the rope. But how to get around? I wasn't in the most convenient position to roll or scoot across the floor.

Once again, I strained at the ropes, ignoring the pain that came with it. And that was when I noticed it. My right ankle was coming loose. Penelope the rodeo clown didn't do as good a job as she thought.

With considerable effort and pain, I wiggled my ankle, and after what seemed like a lifetime of someone hitting my joints with a sledgehammer, I pulled it free. I had one leg free!

Which wasn't much help at all. It was dark, but I bet I looked like the letter *P*. The thought made me giggle. The giggle turned into hysterical laughter. My many concussions were causing me to giggle at the worst times. Like during a piano recital, or wedding, or when you're undercover as a nun at a funeral in Uruguay.

Suddenly it all seemed like one big joke. My life, my relationships, my lack of any sort of job, everything. It didn't matter what happened to me because I was an idiot who put my own life in danger too many times. Eventually the odds got you. Every time.

Like Edna Lou, who was searching for decades for the treasure she thought her ancestor had a claim to—only to find that the gold was in a llama statue in the basement of the old Peters place all along.

Like me, finding out I might be a McMurtry, just like Edna Lou, and a possible descendant of the Peters family. Like Mehitable and Penelope, who looked like me because of a possible family resemblance…

A lightbulb went off in my head. The fog of pain lifted, and I became intensely aware of all the events that led up to this moment.

A lightbulb literally went on overhead as, from my sideways position on the floor, Penelope walked into the room and loomed over me.

"Got a leg free, eh?" She smiled but made no move to retie my ankle.

"Could you just let loose the other one?" I begged. "The pain has me almost losing consciousness—which would be antithetical to your situation."

To my complete surprise, she walked around me, cut the rope, and then lifted me off the floor and set me in a chair.

She pulled up another chair and sat down opposite me.

"That old woman out there"—she pointed at the closed door behind her—"she told me that the rest of the gold is at the police station. And after some persuading, she told me you are engaged to the detective. So, we're going to have a little swap."

"Oh really?" I asked. "Well good luck proving to the police that you have me here. Because I'm not going to say a word."

She narrowed her eyes in confusion. "I wasn't going to have you talk to him. I was just going to take a picture. But now that you said it, that's much better. Proves you're still alive."

"I'm not talking. Do your worst."

Penelope scowled then got up and left the room. I heard mumbling as I looked around. I was in Ike's first house. The one by the zoo. And on the table next to me was the knife Penelope had used to cut my ropes. I picked it up in my mouth and dropped it into the neck of my T-shirt. Then with the grace of a raccoon with unexplainable muscle spasms, I wiggled and moved until the knife was behind me and came out of the middle back of my shirt…and dropped neatly into my hands.

Just in time, too, as Penelope reentered the room and took up her seat across from me. Now, if I could just get her to forget that she left the knife in here, I'd be golden.

The trick was to work on your bonds without flexing enough muscles to give it away. And since it was summer, it was easy to see the muscles in my arms. This would not be easy, but it was all I had.

"Okay, so you really were a spy who can handle anything." She grinned evilly. "But you know who isn't?" She pointed at the door. "You're elderly friend there. Do you want her death on your conscience? I don't think so."

Penelope pulled out her phone and said, "So you will talk, or I will kill your sweet little friend."

I shook my head. "Go ahead."

She looked startled. "What did you say?"

"I said, go ahead and kill her."

The woman stared at me. "I'll do it. I will." But she stayed seated.

"Okay." I sat there and waited.

"You aren't that cold," Penelope said slowly.

I nodded. "That's true. But, I know you won't harm a hair on her head."

Penelope gasped. "Why not?"

I leaned forward conspiratorially. "Because she's your mother. Because you are in this together. Because you both killed Ike."

There was a scream of cold fury at the door, which was flung open to reveal a furious and not-tied-up Edna Lou Murphy. She stormed over to me, her face a mask of rage. This was a version I hadn't seen before.

"How did you know?" She bent down and shrieked into my face.

"Actually, I wasn't one hundred percent sure. Until now, that is." I sat there and smiled at her.

Edna screamed again, and Penelope looked a little alarmed. Edna Lou punched me in the side of the head with an impressive amount of force. I felt a warm trickle run down my face as I kept working the blade, back and forth on the ropes. I would be free in a minute, if only I could stall.

"I'm guessing you had your daughter seduce your cousin, which is *icky* by the way, to find out if he knew anything. When you learned he'd found the gold bars but hadn't told you, and was planning to run off with Penelope, you killed him.

"You faked the attack on you, didn't you?" I accused.

Edna nodded. "I was shooting for a lawsuit on the residents of the old Peters place. My lawyer didn't think I had a chance of getting it, so I thought I'd sue them for assault."

Penelope looked astonished, but her mother's eyes narrowed to slits.

I asked another question. "Why were there six gold bars? I'd have thought all of it would go into making the two-ton llama."

Edna pursed her lips. "Mehitable didn't make the llama. Eustace did. After she died. You were right about that." She smiled. "I didn't give you everything. But Mehitable had kept a couple of bars handy. Ike found them but never told us where."

I looked the old woman in the eye. "You know, I was really rooting for you. I wanted to find that treasure so you could do something big with the Historical Society."

My words seemed to deflate her. The mask of malice slipped from her face, and she looked tired.

"I wanted that too," she said quietly.

Penelope exploded with rage. "What? You said we'd take the money and run off to Costa Rica! You said we'd be rich! You didn't say anything about your stupid society."

The rope was almost severed. I just had to keep them focused on each other and not me.

Edna Lou looked at her daughter. "I know that's what you thought, and I encouraged you to believe it. But the truth was that I wanted to stay here."

Penelope threw her arms up in the air. "You're serious? All the years I'd spent as a child living in a foster family in Des Moines, waiting for you to find the gold and come and get me, was just for this? So you could stay in this stupid town with your stupid Historical Society?"

Her mother snapped, "I'd give you your share! You could do whatever you wanted. I never said you had to stay here!"

The two women squared off, faces grim, fists clenched at their sides. They'd forgotten all about me. Which was good because it made the next part easier.

"Enough!" I shouted as I stood up and pointed the knife at them. "You'll have plenty of time to argue about this in jail."

I reached for my phone, only to find I didn't have it anymore. Penelope turned toward me as Edna Lou held up my cell.

"Looking for this?"

"I have a knife," I said.

Penelope lunged for me. She was taller and heavier than me, but that was about all she had going for her. I stepped aside as she threw herself at me. She landed with a crash on the floor.

I tried to step away, but she grabbed my ankle and yanked. I hit the floor but maintained hold of the knife and slashed out at her. It stuck in her forearm. With a shriek she pulled her arm toward her, and I kicked her.

Edna jumped me as I got up, and began pummeling my head. She was so light that it felt like someone threw a sweater over my shoulders. I reared back and slammed into a wall. It worked because she fell limply to the floor.

Both women lay unconscious as I snatched the phone from Edna Lou's body and with a heavy heart called 9-1-1.

# CHAPTER TWENTY-TWO

———

Rex and Officer Kevin Dooley arrived in minutes. I explained what had happened, and my fiancé arrested each woman as he lifted her to her feet. Backup arrived, and two officers escorted the women back to the station.

"I'm really sorry," I said when we were alone. "I had no intention of doing this. I just went to the cabin to give Edna Lou her stuff back, and Penelope sucker-punched me."

He nodded. "I know. We were actually looking for Edna Lou. Her daughter has a rap sheet a mile long. All petty offenses, but enough. When we traced her foster care records, we found Edna's name."

"You didn't even need my help," I said. "You had solved it yourself."

"It was the fact that Penelope looked like you. I was pretty sure you were related to Edna. The pieces fell into place after that."

"You knew they were in on it together."

Rex gave me a slight smile. "There was always the chance she was doing this to get back at a mother who'd abandoned her to the foster care system. But my gut told me Edna was behind this."

"I know this looks bad." I licked my dry lips. "But I really had no intention of getting involved any further."

He looked at me for a moment. "I know that. This time. But, Merry, this was a rare occasion. Most of the time you don't stop when I've asked you to, and you've almost died multiple times as a result."

I thought about that. "You're right. I'm sorry if I've embarrassed you."

Rex looked away. "No, you haven't embarrassed me. But you've ignored my urging and plowed ahead recklessly in many cases. These dangerous situations are the result of your impulsive behavior."

I sighed. "Where does that leave us?"

"I don't know." He ran his hands through his hair. "I want to marry you, but you keep ignoring my warnings. You're not a spy anymore. You're a civilian. I'm the detective."

Riley's job offer rolled around in my head.

"You still want to marry me?" I squeaked.

He nodded. "Yes. I do. But I don't know how to deal with your impulsiveness."

Kevin stuck his head in the doorway and asked for Rex.

"Go home, Merry," he said. "I'll call you when I have time, and we can talk."

I moped all the way home.

"Edna Lou was in on it?" Kelly asked.

I'd called her, and she'd come right over with her toddler, Finn.

She'd said she had to check for brain damage from three consecutive concussions, before deciding my skull was too thick for any real concern.

"Yup."

"And the meaning of the word *Wubble*?" she asked.

I shrugged. "No idea. I guess we didn't fully wrap up the mystery. But none of this matters because Rex might call the wedding off."

Kelly handed the little girl some Cheerios. Philby came over and supervised the toddler, tolerating her sticky hands as every few seconds she reached out and pulled the cat's whiskers.

"I'm sure he won't do that," Kelly soothed. "You need to work this out."

"What if we can't?" I moaned. "What if this was the last straw?"

My best friend looked me in the eye. "Can you promise to give up these amateur investigations?"

"I want to. But I don't think I can." This was the truth. "It's the only excitement I have, now that I'm a civilian."

"You miss your job, don't you?"

"I do."

We sat there in silence, and I reflected on this. I missed my job. I missed the danger and the thrill of being a spy. I didn't need a therapist to tell me that. And what was worse was that Rex knew I felt this way too.

Kelly sighed. "I think Rex loves you but is finding it hard to deal with your actions."

I was miserable. "I know. You're right."

"I think you might not be quite ready to get married," my matron of honor said.

That hurt.

"What do I do?"

"You need to talk to Rex about all of this." Kelly snagged her daughter as she pried open Philby's lips in an attempt to force-feed the cat a Cheerio. "There's no other solution."

Kelly got to her feet and gathered up her purse and child. "Call me if you need me. But I think this is between you and your fiancé."

I followed her to the door. "You're not going to solve this for me?"

She shook her head. "Not a chance. I'm rooting for you, though." And with that, she was gone.

\* \* \*

Edna Lou had confessed to killing her cousin. I'd heard about it on the news. Not from Rex. A couple of days had passed, and I hadn't seen him, which was something since I live across the street. Susan was out of town dealing with a personal matter, and the zoo had increased its security since the lion incident. Visiting Fancy Pants wasn't an option until I got some new tools.

I spent those days doing what I did best lately—wallow in self-pity. I examined my actions, and while my head knew I'd been a jerk, my heart was thrilled with the excitement. I mean,

I'd almost got eaten by lions, for crying out loud! How cool was that?

Yes, I knew this was the kind of thinking that got me into trouble. No matter how I looked at it, I knew Rex was right. I had no business investigating murders on my own. And yet that was exactly what I wanted to do.

I did spend a whole day on the genealogy website. Turned out I was a descendant of Peggy McMurtry, through her son, Thomas, my great-grandfather. It was something I knew by then, but it was nice to have some evidence. Oh, and on the Wrath side of the family? We were descended from pirates! That was pretty cool. Mom even thought so.

By the third day, Rex texted. He asked me to come over and bring the cats. He'd order pizza. I took this as a good sign and showed up with two bottles of wine (which wasn't easy to juggle with two wriggly beasts).

As we sat at the dining room table with our pizza, I waited for him to speak first. Because I had no idea what he was going to say.

At long last, he spoke up. "Merry, if we're going to make this work, we need to set some parameters."

I stared at him. "Like, rules?" That didn't sound good.

"No, not like rules exactly." He took another slice from the box. "But parameters. I don't want to tie you down with rules. That doesn't seem very healthy for our relationship."

I sat straight up. "We still have a relationship?"

"Yes. We're still engaged," Rex said, "but I think we need to work out some bugs before we get married."

"Okay." I nodded eagerly. "Like what?"

"I think we need to find a way to channel your enthusiasm. I was thinking you might look into getting a job, or something like that."

My mouth dropped open. "A job?"

What could I do that didn't involve guns, knife play, bodies, and secrets?

"Something you'd enjoy. With the new evidence about Mehitable's murder and the solid gold llama the city now owns, the mayor is thinking of making the director of the Historical Society a paid gig."

"You're joking," I said.

He shook his head. "I'm not. Mayor Scott thinks there's some serious tourism potential and is interested in using the old lumber mill to develop a museum."

My heart leapt out of my chest and thudded on the table. Okay, it didn't. But it felt like it.

"It does sound interesting." I didn't know Mayor Scott. In fact, I'd never seen him.

"Did you come up with this idea?" I asked.

Rex smiled. "I might have nudged him in that direction. But seriously, he loved the idea. And he loved the idea that our own hometown hero, Finn Czrygy, would be spearheading it."

I froze. "He knows about me?"

"I'm sorry. Edna Lou was a bit of a gossip. She told half the town."

My anonymity was the best thing about living here. On the other hand, I couldn't have expected it to last forever. And I did see the appeal of having a famous spy running the Who's There museum. But what would people be coming for—history or to gawk at me?

He held up his hands. "I know it's a lot to ask. But just think about it."

"I do love all this local history stuff." I toyed with a pepperoni. "And it would be kind of fun."

"It would only be part-time," Rex said. "Twenty hours a week to start."

"That sounds good…" I said slowly. "I'll think about it."

I was rewarded with a warm smile. "That's all I ask."

We finished dinner with a little canoodling on the couch. Being in Rex's arms made me feel warm. Safe. Unfortunately, I was the biggest danger to myself, and Rex knew it. But as his lips found mine, I was convinced that no matter what my flaws were, he'd always be there for me. This man made me happy. He was smart, wonderful, and left me tingly all over (which was, I should admit, a huge plus.)

We weren't fully okay, but this was a big step. And I was relieved that he still wanted me. I felt a lot better when I headed for home, dragging my cats back across the street.

It was hard to sleep with so many possibilities in my head. Pacing in the living room, I found the card Riley had given me. I must have stared at it for an hour.

When I went to bed, I knew that both men were right. I needed something. And I had two opportunities to figure out what that was, exactly.

I turned out the light, and as I fell asleep, I was, for the first time in a long time, interested in my past *and* my future. And even though that included an ancestral madwoman who was killed by her llama and a fiancé who worried that his bride-to-be would be eaten by lions, the fact of the matter was that my life in the town of Who's There would never, ever be boring.

# ABOUT THE AUTHOR

Leslie Langtry is the *USA Today* bestselling author of the *Greatest Hits Mysteries* series, *Sex, Lies, & Family Vacations*, *The Hanging Tree Tales* as Max Deimos, the *Merry Wrath Mysteries*, the *Aloha Lagoon Mysteries*, and several books she hasn't finished yet, because she's very lazy.

Leslie loves puppies and cake (but she will not share her cake with puppies) and thinks praying mantids make everything better. She lives with her family and assorted animals in the Midwest, where she is currently working on her next book and trying to learn to play the ukulele.

To learn more about Leslie, visit her online at:
http://www.leslielangtry.com

Enjoyed this book? Check out these other reads available in print now from Leslie Langtry:

www.GemmaHallidayPublishing.com